MW00366167

SHE SUFFERED A FRIGHT

Cassie shook her head, confused and exhausted, and she could feel the tears starting again.

"Sh," Phillip said. He rose up on his knees and put his arms around her, drawing her close.

Cassie buried her face in the clean, starched scent of his cravat. She had never felt safer or more cherished in all her life.

He rested his cheek against her hair. "You needn't be frightened, my dear Cassandra. No matter what he wants, he cannot get close to you ever again, I promise."

She wound her arms about his neck and held on as if he were the most precious jewel and she feared someone would snatch him away. . . .

SIGNET

REGENCY ROMANCE
COMING IN MARCH 2003

Mad Maria's Daughter and
The Genuine Article
by Patricia Rice
Two classic Regency romances from the beloved
bestselling author—together in one volume.
"Wicked wit and sizzling sensuality." —Mary Jo Putney

0-451-20824-2

A Foreign Affair
by Evelyn Richardson
Miss Helena Devereaux has just come out for her first
season and fallen for the dashing Major Brett Stanford—
only to find competition from her own mother.

0-451-20826-9

The Indifferent Earl
by Blair Bancroft
Before Abigail Todd can collect her inheritance, she must
honor her grandmother's last wish—to complete a series
of tasks with the Earl of Langley—and hopefully fall in
love in the process.

0-451-20825-0

To order call: 1-800-788-6262

A Loving Spirit

Amanda McCabe

A SIGNET BOOK

SIGNET
Published by New American Library, a division of
Penguin Putnam Inc., 375 Hudson Street,
New York, New York 10014, U.S.A.
Penguin Books Ltd, 80 Strand,
London WC2R 0RL, England
Penguin Books Australia Ltd, 250 Camberwell Road,
Camberwell, Victoria 3124, Australia
Penguin Books Canada Ltd, 10 Alcorn Avenue,
Toronto, Ontario, Canada M4V 3B2
Penguin Books (N.Z.) Ltd, Cnr Rosedale and Airborne Roads,
Albany, Auckland 1310, New Zealand

Penguin Books Ltd, Registered Offices:
Harmondsworth, Middlesex, England

First published by Signet, an imprint of New American Library,
a division of Penguin Putnam Inc.

First Printing, February 2003
10 9 8 7 6 5 4 3 2 1

Copyright © Ammanda McCabe, 2003
All rights reserved

 REGISTERED TRADEMARK—MARCA REGISTRADA

Printed in the United States of America

Without limiting the rights under copyright reserved above, no part
of this publication may be reproduced, stored in or introduced into a
retrieval system, or transmitted, in any form, or by any means (elec-
tronic, mechanical, photocopying, recording, or otherwise), without
the prior written permission of both the copyright owner and the
above publisher of this book.

PUBLISHER'S NOTE
This is a work of fiction. Names, characters, places, and incidents
either are the product of the author's imagination or are used ficti-
tiously, and any resemblance to actual persons, living or dead, business establishments, events, or locales is entirely coincidental.

BOOKS ARE AVAILABLE AT QUANTITY DISCOUNTS WHEN USED TO PROMOTE
PRODUCTS OR SERVICES. FOR INFORMATION PLEASE WRITE TO PREMIUM MAR-
KETING DIVISION, PENGUIN PUTNAM INC., 375 HUDSON STREET, NEW YORK,
NEW YORK 10014.

If you purchased this book without a cover you should be aware that
this book is stolen property. It was reported as "unsold and de-
stroyed" to the publisher and neither the author nor the publisher
has received any payment for this "stripped book."

Chapter One

England, 1811

"Why is it always so *cold* in England?" Cassandra Richards murmured, burrowing deeper into her fur-lined cloak as she watched the Cornwall landscape roll by outside the carriage window.

"I think my toes are frozen," said her friend Antoinette Duvall. "They will never be warm again." Her usually merry coffee-colored face was glum, at odds with her bright red-and-black printed turban.

The two of them sighed, and leaned against each other disconsolately.

Cassie's aunt, Charis, Lady Willowby, called Chat by all her many friends, looked across the carriage at them and shook her head. "You girls! It is only October. There is barely a nip in the air. What are you going to do when it is December and snow is thick on the ground?"

"Snow!" Cassie cried. She had lived for the last fourteen years in hot, sunny Jamaica; she had not seen snow since she was five. All she remembered was that it was very cold and very wet.

And that her father used to make little balls of it, and throw them at her laughing mother.

That memory of her parents, who were now gone and left behind in the small cemetery of their plantation near Negril, gave her a sharp pang. How she missed them! How she missed their life together, a life of sunshine and warm sea.

Even four months in England had not erased her homesickness.

But at least Antoinette had agreed to come with her, she thought, reaching out with the toe of her half boot to nudge the flannel-wrapped brick closer to her friend's feet. Home never seemed quite so far away when she could hear the lilting, musical cadence of Antoinette's voice. And Aunt Chat really *was* trying to make her feel welcome. She had given parties at her house in Bath to introduce Cassie to all her friends, and now she had organized this trip to Cornwall to visit yet another of her friends, the Dowager Lady Royce.

Cassie knew that Aunt Chat hoped that being near the sea would help cheer her up. The least she could do was enjoy it.

She smiled at her aunt. "I cannot wait to see Royce Castle, Aunt Chat! It sounds most intriguing. We don't have buildings that are over five hundred years old in Jamaica."

Chat smiled back. Her pretty, round face was relieved beneath her plumed bonnet. "I am sure you will enjoy it, my dear. My friend Lady Royce is wonderful, and the castle itself most intriguing. There are underground tunnels, secret rooms, and supposedly many ghosts in residence."

Antoinette brightened a bit. "Ghosts, Lady Willowby?"

"Oh, yes. Several, I believe, though I do not know

the details. Melinda or her son should be able to tell you all about it." She shivered a bit. "Though I certainly hope we do not actually *meet* any!"

"Oh, I do!" Cassie said, clapping her gloved hands in delight. "A ghost would be ever so exciting. Did you bring your mother's book of incantations, Antoinette?"

Antoinette was already digging about in her valise. She came up with a thick, worn, brown leather-covered volume. "Of course! I never travel without it. One never knows when one might need an incantation. I also brought some herbs and potions." She pulled a bottle out of the valise, and held it up to the pale sunlight. Small flowers and stems floated about in a clear liquid.

"Wonderful!" Cassie said. "Antoinette's mother was a Yaumumi priestess, Aunt Chat. She taught Antoinette to find all sorts of things that we cannot see. If there *are* any ghosts, she is sure to find them."

Antoinette nodded firmly. "Yes. And if there are unfriendly entities, we shall banish them."

Chat eyed the bottle a bit nervously. "My dears, are you *sure* this is a good idea? Perhaps we should leave the, er, entities alone. We wouldn't like to get them upset, now would we?"

Cassie gave her a reassuring smile. "You mustn't worry, Aunt Chat. Antoinette knows exactly what she is doing. Now, tell me more about your friend. And her son! How very fortunate that they live in such a *spirited* place. They must be terribly interesting people."

"Dearest, I do hope you are going to change your clothes before Lady Willowby and her niece arrive," Melinda Leighton, the Dowager Lady Royce said to her son, when she came into the library on a wave of lilac scent. She proceeded to open the draperies at all the windows, sending sunlight into the gloomy corners of the room.

"What is wrong with what I am wearing, Mother?" Phillip, the Earl of Royce, said distractedly, not even glancing up from the volume he was perusing.

"What is *not* wrong with it? The edges of the coat cuffs are frayed, and is that a hole in the elbow? You should put your new green coat on. And a fresh cravat. You have made ink spots on that one."

Phillip turned over a page. "I will. Later."

"But they will be here at any moment!"

"Surely not. You said they would not be here before teatime."

"It is already past four, dearest."

Phillip did look up then, squinting through his spectacles at the clock on the mantel. "Oh. So it is."

Melinda came over to the desk, and pushed all the piles of books and papers aside to lean over the volume he was reading. "What is it that you find so interesting, Phillip?"

"Thucydides, Mother. It's a very important source for the monograph I'm writing." He marked his place in the volume, closed it, and reached up to remove his spectacles.

"The Pelo-Pelo . . ." Melinda murmured, running one finger over the gilt letters on the book's cover.

"The Peloponnisian War," Phillip said, rubbing at his eyes. He had been working for hours, since just after breakfast, but had not realized at all how late it was growing.

"It sounds horribly depressing," Melinda said. "I am truly glad we are to have some company. You spend far too much time in this room, Phillip. A little society will be good for you."

Phillip leaned back in his chair and smiled up at

her. "Poor Mother. I know it's terribly dull for you here in the wilds of Cornwall, with only my sorry company."

"We were not speaking of me! We were speaking of *you*. Of how excellent it will be for you to be around people for a while."

"I am happy with the way things are. It's very important that I finish my work on the Peloponnesian War; it is a very vital part of my series on ancient Greece."

Melinda shrugged, as usual not listening to her son's obsession with the order and rationality of the ancient world. She was always far more interested in the confusion of the modern world—gossipy letters from her friends, good works at the church, *soirées* on the rare occasions she was in Town.

She went to a mirror on the wall and straightened her cap and her lace shawl. "Nevertheless, dearest, you can take the time to be polite to my friend." She laid her palm against her still-smooth cheek. "I wonder what Chat will think of me. It has been a long time since we saw each other, though I get a letter from her every month. I was much younger then."

"She will think you have not aged a day, because you haven't," Phillip said, coming around to kiss her cheek. "But didn't you say she is also bringing a child with her? I shouldn't think there would be much here to amuse a child."

Melinda laughed. "Her niece is not a child, Phillip! She is eighteen or nineteen, I believe, and she has only just come here from Jamaica. Or maybe Barbados."

Phillip drew back suspiciously. "Eighteen or nineteen? Mother."

She gave him a wide-eyed, innocent look. "What, dearest?"

"You are not matchmaking again, are you?"

"Certainly not! When did I ever play match-maker?"

"When you invited Mrs. Meecham and her daughter to visit. When you invited Lady Bryson and her *four* daughters . . ."

"Oh, well, that. But this is different, Phillip, I assure you. I did not even know that Chat had a niece when I invited her to come here. I am sure the young lady would not be quite suitable, having been out in the West Indies for so long. There is no telling what odd habits she acquired there. Chat writes that she is bringing a very *unusual* companion with her—a native woman! I have never seen a native woman before. And she probably cares nothing for ancient Greece."

"If you say so, Mother," Phillip said, not entirely convinced of her innocence.

Melinda patted his arm reassuringly. "Do not worry, dear. We are going to have a very nice time. Now, I want to go check on the guest chambers just one more time and be sure things are in order. Please, *do* go change your clothes." She turned away to leave the library, then suddenly shivered and drew her shawl closer about her shoulders. "Such a chill! It must be one of the ghosts."

"Mother!" Phillip called after her, exasperated, as she walked away. "I have told you over and over that there is no such thing as ghosts."

"Change your clothes, dear!" she called back blithely.

Phillip watched his mother go, and turned his attention back to his books with a sigh.

He was glad his mother was excited about having guests, truly he was. But why did they have to come to the castle *now*? His work on the new .book was only just beginning. There was so much to be done, and time spent socializing was time wasted away from his work.

And, as his mother pointed out, his wardrobe was hardly up to the fastidious standards of ladies. He ruefully examined a spot of ink on his shirt cuff.

They would just have to take him as he was, he thought as he closed up his books. Perhaps he would not have to see them so very often, after all. Supper and the occasional outing ought to suffice.

Chapter Two

"It *is* very grand, Aunt Chat. Just what a five-hundred-year-old castle ought to look like," Cassie commented, leaning against the carriage window to watch as Royce Castle drew closer and closer.

It was set high above the roiling sea, a great, dark stone sentinel on a craggy bluff. Towers and turrets loomed; windows glinted in the fading sunlight like eyes watching their approach. Not a very welcoming place, certainly. Not at all like the low, bright yellow terraced house she had left in Jamaica. But it was very intriguing.

And it became even more so when Antoinette said, "I feel a great many presences in this house."

Cassie settled back onto the seat. "Truly, Antoinette? All the way from here?"

Antoinette closed her eyes and nodded. "It is very powerful. So many emotions—love, hate, anger, laughter, jealousy. Sudden death."

"How grand," Cassie said happily. "I cannot wait until we arrive and can start our explorations. If, of course, Lady Royce does not mind."

Chat still regarded them rather doubtfully, but she

nodded. "I am sure Melinda will not mind whatever you do. She was always interested in—spiritual inquiry. And I wrote her about Miss Duvall and her unusual activities! But I am not certain about her son."

Cassie laughed. "Oh, yes! The classical scholar. I am very glad you warned us about him, Aunt Chat. Anyone with such a passion for—how did you say it?—order and accuracy would not appreciate our kind of explorations. We shall simply have to be discreet, then, won't we, Antoinette?"

Antoinette gave a warm chuckle.

"Cassandra, my dear, Lord Royce is a brilliant man," Chat admonished. "Everyone in my Philosophical Society says so. His work on the economy and society of ancient Greece is much appreciated."

"Perhaps," Cassandra said doubtfully. "I am sorry, Aunt Chat, but he sounds a rather dull old fellow. One who would not appreciate the great romance of the very house he lives in."

Chat gave an odd little smile. "I think you will not find him to be a dull *old* fellow at all."

Before Cassie could question her aunt about this rather strange statement, the carriage drew to a halt outside the massive front doors of the castle. As they stepped down onto the gravel drive, one of the enormous, nail-studded doors opened and a tiny woman came hurrying out.

She looked like a little Dresden shepherdess in her pink-striped gown and lacy shawl, with silver curls that sprang free from beneath her cap. Her small hands, swathed in lace mitts, fluttered in excitement as she rushed down the stone steps to kiss Chat's cheek.

"My dear friend!" she cried. "Here you are at last. Oh, it has been too long."

"Far too long, Melinda," Chat answered. "I will never forgive myself for not coming to Cornwall sooner."

"Nonsense! You have been so busy, with your niece coming and everything. And this must be her!" Lady Royce turned her fairy-smile onto Cassie. "How do you do, Miss Richards? Why, you are the very image of your aunt when she was a girl!"

Cassie very much doubted that. Aunt Chat was reputed to have been a great beauty, and she was still very handsome. Cassie knew herself to be not much above the ordinary, being short and dark where blonde and willowy was the fashion.

But it was a nice compliment for Lady Royce to pay. Cassie smiled at her in return, and bobbed a small curtsy. "I am very pleased to meet you, Lady Royce. My aunt has told me ever so much about you."

Lady Royce laughed merrily. "Not *too* much, I hope! We did have some larks together when we were girls, didn't we, Chat?" Then her bright eyes slid curiously to Antoinette, who stood a bit behind Cassie, uncharacteristically shy.

"Oh!" Cassie said, reaching for Antoinette's hand to draw her around. "Lady Royce, may I present my companion, Miss Antoinette Duvall?"

"The lady that I wrote to you about," Chat added.

Antoinette curtsied and said in her musical voice, "You have a lovely home, Lady Royce. Very *active*."

Lady Royce clasped her hands together in delight. "Do you mean *spiritually* active, Miss Duvall?"

"Miss Duvall's mother was a, er, priestess," Chat offered. "In Jamaica."

"A Yaumumi priestess," Antoinette answered. "Her gifts were very great. Mine are only a small part of hers, but I sense many entities here."

"Good or bad ones?" Lady Royce asked eagerly.

"I cannot say as of yet," Antoinette said.

Lady Royce nodded. "I have often felt things here, as well, but my son insists there are no ghosts. Oh, but here I have kept you standing about outside when there is a chill in the air! You must all come inside and have some tea. I am very eager to discuss this subject further!"

Lady Royce took Chat's arm and led her through the front doors, the two of them laughing and talking. As Cassie moved to follow them, she glanced up at the house. She thought she saw a movement at one of the upstairs windows, but when she blinked there was no one there. Only a small movement of the draperies.

Phillip watched from his bedroom window as their guests arrived. It was the first time they had had company since Lady Bryson and her daughters almost a year ago, and the household was abuzz with excitement. Most of the servants were gathered in the foyer on one pretext or another, eager to see his mother's friend and her niece and strange companion from the islands.

Phillip was feeling rather reluctantly curious himself.

He had not really wanted them to come. His work was progressing so well, and guests could sometimes be a confounding, demanding nuisance. But his mother had looked so happy when Lady Willowby's letter arrived that he had not had the heart to refuse her.

Now he wondered about these people who were going to be living in his house for the next several weeks.

Lady Willowby was just as his mother had described. Tall, dark-haired, impeccably fashionable in a purple pelisse and feathered bonnet, a printed India shawl about her shoulders. She looked a sensible sort.

A woman stepped out of the carriage after her, swathed from head to toe in a hooded red cloak. This had to be the niece from the West Indies. Phillip had wondered what a girl who had lived most of her life on a tropical island might look like, but it seemed he was not to find out just yet. She was as well-wrapped as any Saracen lady would be.

But then she tipped her head to look up at the house, and her hood fell back.

"Oh!" he said involuntarily. His hands stilled on the cravat he had been attempting to tie.

He wasn't sure what he had been expecting, but not this pretty woman. Her hair was black and shining as a raven's wing, parted sleekly in the middle and drawn back to a simple low knot at the nape of her neck. No fashionable curls or whorls marred the sheen of it, and its only ornament was a carved comb of some dark wood.

Her skin was smooth and faintly sun-touched, over high cheekbones and a slightly pointed chin. A pair of long, sparkling earrings swung against her cheeks and caught in the rich sable lining of her hood.

She smiled as she surveyed the house, as if pleased with its aspect, and Phillip found himself quite pleased himself that she should like it. He wondered if she would like *him* as well . . .

Then he realized what he was thinking and frowned. "Fool!" he muttered, his hand crushing his cravat.

He was meant to be thinking of his work, not watching a pretty lady out of windows and wondering if she would like him. That was for men who had nothing better to do, society fribbles who just sat about at their clubs and danced at balls.

Even as he thought this, he could not stop himself from looking at the elf-girl again. She was half-turned away, talking to another woman. This other woman was a very interesting vision, indeed. She was quite tall, perhaps as tall as his own six feet, with dark, gleaming skin. She wore an odd pelisse-robe of crimson and black, with a matching turban concealing her hair. She, too, surveyed the house, with narrowed, assessing eyes. Then she said something to the woman in the cloak and nodded.

Well, this *was* quite interesting. Phillip's scholarly mind was turning, coming up with countless questions he would like to ask these ladies about their lives in the West Indies. It must have been a fascinating existence, full of old-fashioned superstitions and myths.

It was simply too bad they were not Greek. What a great help *that* would have been to his work.

"My lord?" his long-suffering valet said from behind him.

Phillip turned to see that he held out his best coat, the dark green superfine his mother had insisted he wear, the one with only one small hole on the sleeve. "Yes, Jones?"

"Your mother has sent a message saying the guests have arrived," Jones said, holding the coat out farther with a rather hopeful air. "She asks that you join them in the drawing room, my lord, at your earliest convenience."

"Yes, of course. Mustn't be late," Phillip murmured. He glanced back out the window, but everyone had already gone inside.

Chapter Three

Cassie munched on a tea cake and examined all the portraits lining the walls of the vast drawing room. They were varied and very fascinating, ranging from a Renaissance gentleman in a velvet cap and cloak to a picture hung over the fireplace of the present Lady Royce as a young bride. She cocked her head to one side to examine the portrait of a Restoration lady with blond curls and a blue satin gown.

The lady in turn seemed to move her head to examine Cassie.

"Such an engaging family you have, Lady Royce," Cassie said, straightening her head. Now the lady appeared to be staring out vacantly into space. "I would love to hear about each and every portrait."

Lady Royce gave a pleased little laugh. "I will be happy to tell you all you wish to know, my dear Miss Richards! Though of course they are not exactly *my* family, I feel as if they are, since I married into the Leighton family when I was only sixteen." She paused to refill Antoinette's teacup and pass Chat another sandwich, then went on, "That portrait you are looking at is Louisa, Lady Royce. She came to a rather bad end. She fell off the cliffs into the sea."

Antoinette examined the painting. "I believe she still dwells in the East Tower."

Lady Royce looked at her with wide, wondering eyes. "So I have heard. I personally have not seen her, or the knight who walks about in his armor. And then there is our most famous ghost, Louisa's husband's great-grandmother Lady Lettice."

Cassie looked over where Lady Royce indicated to see a painting of a woman in Elizabethan regalia, ruff, drum farthingale, and ropes of pearls and rubies.

Antoinette frowned. "I cannot sense her presence."

"No one has seen her in quite a long time," Lady Royce said regretfully. "Not since before I came to live here. But there are many legends about her. They say she cannot find peace because she was betrayed by her true love."

"We shall just have to find her, then, won't we, Antoinette?" Cassie said.

Antoinette nodded slowly. "Perhaps."

"Well, if I can be of any help, do let me know," said Lady Royce. Then she looked past the settee where Cassie and Antoinette sat, and smiled. "Phillip, dear, here you are at last! Do come and greet our guests."

Cassie put down her teacup and placed a polite smile on her face, preparing to greet the shambling scholar, whom she still pictured as old despite his mother's youthful appearance. She didn't hear any tap of a cane on the floor, or smell any camphor to warn of his approach.

She stood and turned around, and felt the polite smile freeze on her lips.

Why, Lord Royce was not old at all! In fact, he did

not look much like her idea of a scholar, as he was quite good-looking. He was a trifle thin, true, especially compared to the burly, broad-shouldered planters she was accustomed to at home. And his complexion was rather pale, probably from spending a great deal of time studying indoors. His eyes were an intense, stormy gray, that seemed to pierce right through to her innermost soul.

But she would have thought him a poet, not a student of antique civilizations. His hair was not just in need of a bit of a trim, it was truly unfashionably long, falling almost to his shoulders in thick dark brown waves, as if he could not be bothered to cut it. It was damp, as if he had just washed it and hastily combed it back, but it was rich and soft-looking. She actually lifted her hand a bit, wanting to touch it, before she realized what she was doing and dropped her arm back to her side.

No, Lord Royce was not at all what she had been expecting!

Then Lady Royce's voice came to her through the haze, and she realized that things had been going on about her. Things she ought to pay attention to, such as introductions.

". . . and this is her niece, Miss Cassandra Richards," Lady Royce was saying.

Cassie stared dumbly at Lord Royce as he reached for the hand she had dropped to her side, and lifted it to his lips for a brief salute.

His breath was warm on her fingers, and she had to fight down the strong urge to giggle. She scarcely even noticed the small hole in his green sleeve.

"I am pleased to make your acquaintance, Miss Richards," he said. "I suppose you must always speak the truth?" His voice was dark and rich, like Jamaican rum.

Cassie blinked at him. What on earth was the man talking about? "Ex-excuse me, Lord Royce?"

He smiled at her as one would to a rather slow child. "Your name. Cassandra. 'Disbelieved by men.' Are you named after the great prophetess of Troy?"

Cassie vaguely remembered her mother telling her the story of the Trojan Cassandra, who was doomed to always tell the truth of her prophecies and never be believed. Her mother had loved the old myths. "I suppose I must be," she answered.

He gave her another smile, and went to sit beside his mother. Cassie slowly sat back down, her mind screaming one word at her. "Fool, fool, fool!"

She could feel her face flaming. What a thorough idiot he must think her!

"Miss Richards was just asking me about the history of the castle," Lady Royce said, pouring out a cup of tea for her son. "She is very interested in it."

Lord Royce raised his dark brow at Cassie. "Indeed, Miss Richards?"

Cassie seized on the topic. Surely she could converse more easily about a haunted castle than ancient Troy. "Oh, yes! It is truly fascinating. There must be much to learn about it."

"It *is* an interesting place," he agreed. "I plan to someday write a history of it. It was built in 1320, by the first Earl of Royce . . ."

"I believe she is more interested in Lady Lettice, the knight, and Louisa, dear," interrupted Lady Royce.

That dark brow rose again. "Is that what you are interested in, Miss Richards? The so-called ghosts?"

Cassie frowned, but before she could reply, Antoinette said, "You are a disbeliever, Lord Royce."

"I suppose I am," answered Lord Royce. "I prefer

the logic and rationality of ancient Greece to spooks
and haunts."

"Hmm," Antoinette murmured, surveying him
through narrowed ebony eyes.

Lord Royce fidgeted a bit under her steady gaze,
and turned away to address a question to Aunt Chat.

Cassie studied him over the rim of her teacup.
Well, he might be handsome as a poet, but he was
obviously quite as obnoxiously *logical* as she had
feared he might be.

Chapter Four

"I liked Lady Royce, didn't you, Cassie?" Antoinette asked. The two of them were in Cassie's room before they retired, to brush each other's hair and talk over the day. After they had convinced some rather snooty upper servants that Antoinette was Cassie's friend and not her maid, she had been given the chamber next door to Cassie's. Just like at the house in Jamaica.

"Yes, very much," Cassie answered, reaching for a strand of her freshly brushed hair to braid. "She was all that was charming. And she agreed to give us a tour of the castle tomorrow. That should be most interesting."

"Perhaps we can find Lady Lettice!"

"Perhaps so. And Louisa and the armored knight. I don't think Lady Royce's son would very much appreciate us going on a ghost hunt, though," Cassie murmured. She thought of Lord Royce, of his poet's hair and his mysterious gray eyes, of the smoky roughness of his voice.

Of that obnoxious raised brow, proclaiming how silly he thought her.

She frowned.

"Oh, yes. Lord Royce," Antoinette said. "He does not believe. He does not sense all that is around him. It is very sad."

Cassie felt a strange urge to defend Lord Royce, even with the memory of his scoffing in her mind. "Not everyone is as sensitive as you, Antoinette. Not everyone can so easily believe in things they cannot touch or see. Or read in dusty books, as Lord Royce does."

"*You* believe."

"I am different from most of the English we have met. I lived in Jamaica, where things are very—different." Cassie turned her head to look out the uncurtained window, where all the autumn stars shimmered.

Usually she was happy enough here in England. Her aunt had been all that was kind, and life at Chat's house in Bath was very comfortable. But sometimes, especially in unguarded moments like these, she felt like such an outsider. Like she could never possibly understand the people around her, nor they her. She did not understand the things they took for granted, and they often thought her an oddity.

Just as Lord Royce had.

She would feel completely alone all the time, were it not for Antoinette. But she sometimes felt guilty for bringing her here, where, if Cassie felt like an oddity, Antoinette must feel ten times more so. She had faced shocked looks and fierce whispers ever since they reached England.

She turned to Antoinette, and asked, as she had a dozen times before, "Do you not miss home?"

Antoinette paused in braiding her thick mane of wavy hair, and gave the same answer she always gave. "Of course I do. Just as you do, Cassie. It is the only home I have ever known. But I would have missed you far more, if you had left without me."

"Truly?"

"What did I have left in Jamaica? My mother is dead. Since I grew up with you and was educated, I do not fit in with my own people. You are like a sister to me. How could I let you go off into the world alone?"

Cassie blinked at the sudden prickle of tears at her eyes. She wiped at them with the sleeve of her dressing gown. "Just as you are like my sister! I only hope you will never be sorry for your decision."

Antoinette dabbed at her own tears. "I will not. But if I do, I can always go back. It is a long way, but not impossible. Just as you could go back, Cassie, and marry that awful Mr. Bates. He did offer for you before we left."

Cassie laughed at the memory of Mr. Bates, pressing his suit on her just as she was about to board the ship to England. "So he did! Though I daresay life at Aunt Chat's home in Bath is far preferable to life as Mrs. Bates. And we would have missed seeing this lovely castle!"

"Indeed we would have," Antoinette said, the lilting humor back in her voice. "Speaking of which, we have much to do tomorrow. Shall we retire?"

Cassie shook her head. "You go ahead. I am not tired yet."

Antoinette frowned in concern. "Do you want me to find you some warm milk?" Cassie had had some trouble sleeping since coming to England, and Antoinette and Aunt Chat tried everything to help her. Nothing really seemed to work.

"No, I think I'll go to the library and look for a book," Cassie answered. "Lady Royce said I could borrow any of them I like, though I must say her son looked rather doubtful about it. He probably thinks I will put all his precious volumes out of order!''

Antoinette laughed. "Very well," she said, walking toward the door. "Just be certain you don't choose one of those horrid novels you are so fond of. They always give you bad dreams."

"I won't. Good night, Antoinette."

"Good night, Cassie."

Once her friend was gone, Cassie slid her feet into her bedroom slippers and lit a candle to carry down to the library.

Royce Castle seemed different in the lonely night darkness, eerie and echoing. The main staircase, a winding, wide expanse of stone, had been covered with a long Aubusson carpet runner and decorated with tall candelabra and statuary, but it was still cold and dark. Her candle flickered in a sudden draft, sending shadows dancing on the walls. The wind whistled around the edges of the narrow windows, and made the tapestries flutter.

It sounded like high-pitched laughter. And did that portrait just *wink* at her?

Cassie cautiously lifted her candle higher to peer at the painted image. Obviously the wink had just been a trick of the light, thank goodness. She did want to see a ghost, but maybe not when she was all alone.

She hurried her steps along. Once she reached the library, she was so relieved to be there that she slammed the door behind her and leaned back against it. She closed her eyes, listening to the swift patter of her heart.

"May I help you?" a deep voice said.

Cassie's eyes flew open, and she stood up perfectly straight. Lord Royce sat behind a massive, carved desk set half in the shadows, books and papers piled around him in untidy heaps. Light from the blazing fire in the hearth fell across him in a red-gold glow, burnishing his rich fall of hair and glinting off the spectacles he wore.

Cassie felt oddly breathless, and she had the sneaking suspicion that it had nothing to do with ghosts or shadows.

"L—Lord Royce," she managed to gasp. "I had no idea anyone would be here. The lateness of the hour . . ."

"It *is* rather late. I would have thought you would be quite tired, Miss Richards, after your journey." He rose from behind the desk, and Cassie saw that he was in his shirtsleeves, his waistcoat unbuttoned and his cravat untied and carelessly dangling. She even had a glimpse of his strong throat, and the hollow at its base where his pulse beat, as he walked toward her.

She had lived a rather casual life in Jamaica, had seen her father and other planters come in from the fields dressed in very similar fashion. But she had never been so disconcerted by it before. She was not quite certain where to look as he moved closer and closer.

He stopped what seemed like mere inches from her, so close that she could feel his warmth, could smell the faint scent of some spicy soap on his skin. She forgot to breathe entirely when he reached his arm behind her, the fine cambric of his sleeve brushing against her hair.

He took his coat from the hook that was on the door she had just been leaning against, and slid his arms into the sleeves. He stepped away from her, pulling his hair from under the collar in one smooth motion.

"Are you not, Miss Richards?" he said.

The sound of his voice seemed to shake her from some sort of dream state. Then she realized that the entire process of him moving across the library, which had seemed to take hours, had only taken a moment.

"Am I not what?" she murmured, confused.

And there went that blasted eyebrow. "Tired after your journey."

"Not at all." She moved away from him, crossing the wide expanse of the room to be closer to the fireplace. She was suddenly all-too-aware that she was clad in her nightclothes. She pulled the edges of her velvet dressing gown closer together and wished she was still in her dinner gown. "I wanted to find something to read."

"Well, we certainly have plenty of that," he said, gesturing to the massive bookcases. "What do you care for, Miss Richards? History? Biography? Sermons?"

"Do you have any novels? Recent novels," she said without thinking, then immediately regretted it. She felt like a fool asking a classical scholar for novels.

But his brow did not arch at all. "Of course. I believe you will find most of them here. Many of them are my mother's, which she orders from London every month." He showed her a smaller case, placed against the wall near the desk.

As Cassie came closer to inspect them, her attention was caught by the clutter on the desk. A large sheaf of paper, closely written in a small, neat hand, balanced beside a stack of leather-bound volumes. *His* handwriting, *his* work, she realized.

She was suddenly intensely curious as to what it was that so preoccupied this strange, beautiful man. She veered off her course and went over to gently touch one of the books.

"What is it you are working on, Lord Royce?" she asked. "My aunt and her Philosophical Society in Bath are great admirers of your writing."

"I am flattered," he said, moving closer. "I am working on a series about the wars of ancient Greece, which will follow my series on society and economy. This one concerns the Peloponnesian War, between Athens and Sparta."

Cassie nodded and turned some of the books over in her hands, reading the titles by Aristotle, Pausanias, Xenophon.

They made her feel terribly ignorant.

Then she saw something a bit more familiar, a slim volume titled *The Gods and Goddesses of Ancient Greece*. She picked it up and flicked through the illustrated pages.

"My mother adored the myths and tales of Greece and Rome," she said. "She died when I was eleven, but I remember her telling me some of these stories."

She looked up to find Lord Royce watching her intently with his gray eyes, uncovered now by the spectacles. She gave a nervous little laugh and placed the book carefully back on its stack. "I am sorry," she said. "I did not mean to mess about with your books."

He shrugged. "It is of no matter. You can read any of them you choose, Miss Richards. So your mother was a scholar of the classics?"

Cassie laughed to think of her sociable, party-loving mother as any kind of scholar. "Oh, no! Not a bit. She was far too busy with routs and fetes to study. She just enjoyed the stories. Perhaps because the ancient gods so enjoyed a good party themselves!"

He laughed at her little quip, and she found herself grinning like an idiot that she could make him laugh.

"Then I am surprised she did not name you after someone more lighthearted than Cassandra," he said. "Aphrodite, perhaps, or Psyche."

He leaned forward to straighten the pile of books, and a long lock of dark hair fell forward over his face. Cassandra had the strangest urge to brush it back, to see if it was as silky as it looked.

"There must have been something about Cassandra that appealed to her darker side," she answered distractedly. "What did you say it meant? Disbelieved by men?"

He smiled at her wryly. "Much to the men's peril."

She smiled at him in return, feeling a faint warm glow. Perhaps he was not such a stuffy prig after all, she mused. "I should like to hear more of Cassandra's story."

"Then I shall tell it to you one day soon. It is a very good tale."

"I would like that."

"And perhaps in return you could answer a few questions about Jamaica, Miss Richards? One in particular, though I fear it is rather prying."

Cassie positively burned with curiosity to know what it might be. "Yes, Lord Royce?"

"Your friend Miss Duvall. Is she your slave?"

She stared at him, more deeply offended than she could ever remember being before. All the warm camaraderie of only moments before blew away like so many cold ashes. "Of course she is not my slave! She is a free woman, as was her mother. Her mother came to work as my mother's lady's maid soon after we arrived in Jamaica, and she became a dear friend. When she died, Antoinette stayed with us, as my companion. We grew up together, and she is like my sister." She glared at him, daring him to contradict her.

He held up his hands, as if in surrender. "Miss Richards! My deepest apologies. I never meant to offend."

Cassie looked at him rather suspiciously, but he seemed sincere. She nodded and said, "My father owned no slaves. All his workers were freed men whom he paid wages. It meant that his endeavors were not as profitable as those of some of his neighbors, but he did the right thing, and I was very proud of him."

"As well you should be, Miss Richards," he said in a soft, respectful tone she had not heard him use before. "He sounds quite admirable, and I am truly sorry for being so flippant."

"Apology accepted, then, Lord Royce."

"How can I make amends for being such a dolt?"

"Well . . ." Cassie said, pondering this question carefully. "You can tell me about the castle's ghosts, as well as about Cassandra."

He shook his head. "I fear my mother is the expert on ghosts. I know little about the stories."

"But you live right here in the castle!" Cassie said, unable to fathom that someone could be so completely uninterested in the spirits around them. "Aren't you the least bit curious about them?"

"I have more important work to do, Miss Richards, than chase 'ghosts' about." He picked up a book from a nearby shelf, *Letter to a Member of the National Assembly* by Edmund Burke. "Burke says, 'Superstition is the religion of feeble minds.' "

Cassie wrinkled her nose. "He sounds a most dull fellow."

"He was one of the greatest thinkers of the last century."

"Was he indeed?" she murmured, unconvinced. "Perhaps I should read him, then, after I have toured the castle and met every spirit in residence."

"Perhaps you should, Miss Richards. Perhaps you should."

Cassie felt faintly disappointed. Their conversation had been going so well, until he asked her about Antoinette and then dismissed the ghost stories out of hand. Now he only seemed the stuffy scholar again, watching her with that doubtful look on his face. As if he had some reservations about her sanity.

She pulled a couple of novels off the shelf in order to fulfill her original errand, and, clutching them against her, turned toward the door. "It is getting very late, Lord Royce. I will say good night."

"Good night, Miss Richards," he replied, giving her a small bow. "It was a most interesting conversation."

"Indeed it was," she said quietly. Then she hurried out of the dimly lit haven of the library and back up the cold stone stairs.

She was so distracted that she did not even notice the drafts and the portraits this time. Indeed, she thought of nothing but the strange Lord Royce until her head fell onto her pillow and she dropped into a dream-filled sleep.

Chapter Five

Phillip sat alone in the library long after Cassandra left, long after the embers faded in the fireplace and a late-night chill crept in from the tall windows.

What a very odd young woman Miss Cassandra Richards was. She did not behave as any other young lady of his acquaintance did. She did not shriek and scurry away when she found him there in the library, even though it was quite an improper situation. She did not back away from his questions about life in Jamaica. Instead, she faced him directly and unflinchingly, not at all awed by his title or position.

Very unusual.

Phillip gave a little, self-mocking laugh. His experience with well-bred young ladies was admittedly not wide. He escorted his mother to Town when the occasion warranted. He squired her about to stultifying Society balls, and met with his publisher and other scholars. He enjoyed the discussions and debates, but could distinctly do without the balls.

All the young ladies there would cluster about him like so many pastel-clad butterflies, giggling and chattering on about fashions and parties. It gave him a headache just thinking about the superficial chaos of it all.

He always felt such an outsider at those occasions, as if he were speaking a different language from the people around him, and he longed to be home at Royce Castle, with his books and studies.

He knew very well that one day he would have to marry, to carry on the family line and add to the portraits that clustered on every wall. But he had always imagined he would find a sensible woman when the time came, a widow or spinster bluestocking, who could share his interest in antiquity and bring up equally sensible children.

Miss Richards was obviously *not* a sensible bluestocking by any stretch of the imagination. She did not know much about classical history, nor did she scruple to admit her interest in the so-called supernatural. She had worn a most daring gown of canary-yellow satin to supper, along with dazzling beaded earrings and a carved stone pendant. She had chattered brightly with his mother about ghosts and popular novels.

All the things he usually so disliked. But he had *not* been bored in the least. Rather, he had been quite fascinated and had wanted to listen to her more, to lean closer to her and breathe deeply of her exotic perfume.

It was all most odd. It he were to subscribe to the ideas of Miss Richards, her enigmatic friend Miss Duvall, and his mother, he would say he was under a spell.

But more likely it was the lateness of the hour, he thought, as the clock struck three. And the fact that he had been working so hard of late. It was making him tired and distracted. Perhaps his mother was right. Company would do him some good.

He would just have to spend more time with Miss
Richards—and Lady Willowby and Miss Duvall, of
course—and see if that helped cure these fancies. No
doubt once he spent more time with Cassandra Richards, her exotic appeal would wear off and his life
would return completely to normal. No more talk
of ghosts, no more rich perfumes, just ancient wars
and philosophy.

On that comforting thought, he closed his books,
blew out the candles, and left the library for bed.

Two unseen "people," perched atop the rolling library ladders, watched him go with great interest.

"Oh, this *is* going to be amusing!" said Louisa,
twisting one long, golden ringlet about her finger.
"He is infatuated with that girl already and will not
admit it."

"He cannot admit it," Sir Belvedere said, his armor
clanking as he turned a page over in the book he was
perusing. If Phillip had still been in the library, he
might have looked up to see a volume floating about
in midair, but he would have put it down to fatigue
or a bad cheese at dinner. Just as he always did.

This amused Sir Belvedere and Louisa to no end,
brightening their endless days and nights in the castle. And now it looked as if the amusement was
about to increase.

"I like that Miss Richards and her tall, strange
friend. I should not have been so mischievous about
making the portrait move, when they are so very
nice!" said Louisa in a most chagrined tone. "They
believe in us; they know we are here."

"Not as of yet, my fair lady. But they will know
when we reveal ourselves to them." Sir Belvedere's
visor fell with a loud thud over his face, and he
pushed it aside impatiently.

"Oh, no!" Louisa answered, fluffing up her lace-trimmed blue satin skirts. "They already know, I am certain. And they will soon make that stubborn Lord Royce see. Why, he is every bit as obstinate as my husband was!"

Sir Belvedere chuckled. "It will be vastly amusing to watch them try to make him see, Louisa. *Vastly* amusing. 'Twill be the most enjoyment I have had since I overran castles in my mortal life!"

"It is simply too bad Lady Lettice is not here to see this. She was always so wonderful at matchmaking, at helping people to see how perfect they are for each other. Do you remember what she did for this Lord Royce's grandfather and that Miss Sutcliffe?" Louisa smiled at the memory. "I think Lord Royce and Miss Richards will need a great deal of help as well."

"I, too, miss Lady Lettice," said Sir Belvedere. "It has been a long while since we saw her. But if anything can bring her back, it is two people falling reluctantly in love."

Chapter Six

Cassie awoke from a dream of Jamaica, of walking along a warm, sandy shore with the bright morning sun shining down on her, to find herself not sun-bathed and cozy but chilled and shivering. Sometime during the restless night she had thrown off the bed-clothes, and her bare feet stuck out into the cold room.

"Wretched!" she muttered, yanking the blankets back up over her shoulders and rolling over onto her side. The fire was long-dead in the grate, but the draperies at the window were drawn partially back, letting a bar of yellow-white sunlight fall across the floor.

The room was so quiet that she could hear, very faintly, the rush and roar of the sea, far below the cliffs. It reminded her of her dream, and drew her out from the warm cave of the bed. She slid her feet into her slippers and padded over to look out the window.

She *could* see the sea, but it was not like the violet-blue waters of the island. It was gray, almost black, roiling angrily against the steep cliffs beyond the castle's manicured gardens. The sun that was struggling so valiantly through the slate-colored clouds did not even seem to penetrate them at all. Scrubby trees grew along the cliffs, bending gaunt limbs toward the sea like hands in the wind.

Cassie had never felt so far from home before. She shivered and crossed her arms tightly in front of her.

Then, out of the starkness, she saw a flash of movement. A figure on horseback riding along the cliffs, sweeping past the trees and creating a veritable whirlwind of energy.

He was quite a distance away, but she could see the banner of dark hair that flowed in the wind.

Lord Royce.

Cassie had decided when she went to bed that he was just a fusty scholar after all, interested only in his books, but he certainly did not look *fusty* this morning.

He looked like a dashing poet. Or a pirate, against the backdrop of that dark sea. He rode along fast and furious, his horse's hooves churning up the earth. His white shirt billowed, adding to the illusion of piracy.

Cassie smiled. Perhaps her strange fascination with him was not so odd after all.

There was a quick knock at the door, dashing these fanciful thoughts. Cassie turned away from the window and called, "Come in."

Antoinette entered the room, majestic in a blue-and-green swirl of a gown and a matching turban. Despite the early hour, she looked rested and regal, as usual.

"Cassie!" she tsked. "Here it is time for breakfast, and you're not dressed."

"I did not sleep restfully," Cassie said with a little shrug. "I had such odd dreams."

Antoinette came up beside her and peered over

her shoulder out the window. Lord Royce was just disappearing from view, his hair still flowing in the wind. "Um-hm," she murmured. "And I see what those dreams were about."

"Antoinette!" Cassie cried, jerking the draperies closed. "It was not like that at all. Lord Royce is not even my sort of gentleman. He is—is narrow-minded, and cares only for books, and . . ." She struggled to remember what it was she had not liked about him, but the image of him riding along the cliffs kept interfering.

Antoinette laughed. "And just what *is* your sort of gentleman? Men like the ones back in Jamaica?"

"Yes!" Cassie said firmly. She went over to the dressing table and picked up her hairbrush, pulling it through her hair and detangling the night's plait.

"Planter sorts?" Antoinette's voice was sardonic, her accent thick.

"Yes," Cassie repeated, but more doubtful this time. Antoinette made her remember how some of those men had truly been, careless and unrefined, caring only about getting foxed on rum.

"Then why did you not accept Mr. Bates' proposal?" Antoinette teased. "With his big plantation and all. Why, he would be just your sort."

Cassie laughed, acknowledging the truth of her friend's words. "Oh, all right! So they were *not* my sort. But neither is Lord Royce."

"Is he not?"

"No. I wouldn't think *you* would like him, either; he doubts your sight. And why are we talking about this at all? I'm not interested in finding a suitor here. I am interested only in the ghosts."

Antoinette nodded. "Then you should hurry up and get dressed. Lady Royce is going to give us a tour of the castle after breakfast, and tell us all the tales."

"What fun!" Cassie cried, and ran over to the armoire to find a morning dress. "I presume her son will *not* be joining us."

So she would be able to enjoy herself without the distraction of his presence.

"Presumably," Antoinette agreed. "But you must bear up under the disappointment, Cassie. I am sure you will see him at supper; I foresaw it in the cards."

Cassie threw a pillow at Antoinette, who just ducked and laughed.

"That particular Lady Royce, Louisa was her name, had a very sad history," Lady Royce said, enthusiastically spreading marmalade on her toast. "Very sad indeed. Her husband left her alone here at Royce Castle while he fought in the Civil War, and even when the king came back he was away at Court often. They say Louisa took a lover in her loneliness, but he betrayed her, and she threw herself off the cliffs in despair."

"What fustian!" Louisa muttered, peering down from her perch atop a decorative cornice in the breakfast room. "I was in my cups after that ball, and *fell* off the cliffs."

"Ha!" scoffed Lord Belvedere, his armor clanking.

"It is true! No lover ever betrayed me."

"Methinks, fair lady, that the years have clouded your memory. I was right here, as I have been for almost five hundred years, and I saw you that night. You were indeed 'in your cups,' but if you had not quarreled with that Lord Ponsonby and gone running down to the cliffs . . ."

"Oh, hush!" Louisa interrupted, reaching out a hand and shoving him off his own cornice. "I want to hear what else she has to say."

"What was that clattering noise?" said Lady Royce, her toast held up halfway to her mouth.

Antoinette looked directly at Sir Belvedere, causing him to gasp and vanish altogether, leaving only Louisa high on her perch.

"Probably only one of your footmen," said Chat. "Now, what were you saying about the sad Louisa?"

"Sad, hmph," whispered Louisa. "I am *happy*."

"Oh, she is not sad," said Antoinette, taking a serene sip of her chocolate.

"Exactly," Louisa agreed.

"Perhaps once she was, but now she enjoys her existence here."

"She is here, then?" Cassie said eagerly. "You can feel her presence? Can we find her?"

"Really, Cassie," said Chat. "It is too early in the morning for hauntings and ghosts and such."

"And everyone knows that midnight is the time for such endeavors," a deep male voice said from the doorway.

Everyone's gaze, including Louisa's, turned to Lord Royce. She eyed him with some approval; he looked a bit like her husband, William, who had not been an unhandsome man by any means. But this Lord Royce, like her William, was bent on his own ends, which left little time for romance. With William it had been advancement at Court, with this man it was his studies.

Oh, the great folly of men! They never learned, not even in over a hundred years. With a rueful shake of her head, Louisa vanished, gone to seek other amusement in the East Tower.

Antoinette watched her go with narrowed eyes, but Cassie was far too distracted by the presence of Lord Royce to notice any ghostly doings.

He had obviously bathed and changed after his

ride, for he was respectably, albeit a bit shabbily, attired in a blue morning coat and buff breeches, his hair tied neatly back. The wild pirate was gone, and the scholar/earl firmly in his place.

But Cassie still felt flustered and flushed when he looked at her.

"Good morning, ladies," he said, sitting down in the last vacant chair, the one across from Cassie.

Her fork clattered against her plate, and she had to catch it before it fell to the floor.

He smiled at her. "I trust you all found your first evening at Royce Castle to be comfortable?"

"Yes, quite," Chat answered. "It was all that Melinda has written me over the years. Splendid."

"I slept quite soundly," said Antoinette. "Although next door there were some rather restless noises . . ."

Cassie kicked her under the table.

"The butler told me you went riding this morning, dear," said Lady Royce. "You were awake unusually early." She turned to Chat and added, "Ordinarily my son is up quite late with his studies and doesn't join me for breakfast."

"It must be the bracing autumn air," he answered, spearing one of the sausages on his plate. "It was a lovely morning for a ride."

"Indeed," said Lady Royce. "Do *you* ride, Miss Richards?"

Cassie blinked at her, startled to be suddenly addressed. "Yes, Lady Royce. A bit. But I fear I have not had much opportunity for it since I came to England."

"Bath is rather restrictive for poor Cassandra," said Chat.

Cassie smiled at her aunt. "Now, Aunt Chat! I *like* living in Bath. The theater, the concerts . . ."

"But very few places for riding," said Chat.

"Perhaps you would care to ride while you are here, then," Lady Royce said. "We have such a nice stable, and Phillip knows all the best paths. I am sure he would enjoy showing them to you."

Then, Lady Royce and Chat exchanged little smiles, and simultaneously lifted their teacups to their lips for demure sips.

Cassie clasped her hands tightly on her lap, twisting her napkin, and looked across the table at Lord Royce. Surely he would refuse to go riding with her, would scoff at his mother's obvious scheming. What would they ever find to talk about on their ride? What could they have in common?

But, to her surprise, he looked rather—amenable.

"*Would* you care to go riding with me, Miss Richards?" he said, his face smoothly polite.

Would she? Cassie remembered the vision of him she had seen from her window, all dashing and piratical. Then she imagined herself by his side, riding free in the wind, just as she had at home.

Of course she would *like* to go riding with him, but whether she *should* was something else. It would be far too easy to forget their differences out there in the sunshine.

And, as she had no intention of falling in love with a man so very serious-minded, forgetting those differences would not be good. She ought to refuse . . .

"Yes, thank you, Lord Royce," she heard herself say. "I would enjoy that."

He gave her a startled little smile, as if surprised that she had agreed. "Very good. Perhaps we could inspect the stables later and find you a suitable horse."

"After I show them the East Tower, dear," said Lady Royce. "They want to see where poor Louisa's chambers are."

He rolled his eyes a bit. "Of course. And you can play a game of piquet with her while you are there. Do you think she would care for a sherry? There is a fine Amontillado in the cellar."

Obnoxious man! Cassie fumed in her mind, turning her attention back to her plate. And to think she had agreed to go riding with him.

Chapter Seven

"This is the East Tower, where Louisa lived," Lady Royce said, unlocking a door and leading them up a narrow staircase. "I seldom come here; with just Phillip and myself in residence there are many rooms that are unused. But I promised you a look at them, so here we are! What do you all think?"

"Very pretty," Chat said.

"Very," agreed Cassie, looking about her. The round tower room was large and high-ceilinged, furnished in the style of almost two hundred years ago, with a massive carved bed and looped draperies at the tall windows. Another portrait hung over the marble fireplace of Louisa and a stern-faced man with long dark hair.

He looked a bit like the current Lord Royce, Cassie thought. She went over to take a closer look.

There was a gilt-framed mirror next to the painting, and Cassie thought she saw a brief flash of blue in the glass. But when she glanced over her shoulder, there was no one there who should not be. Only Aunt Chat and Antoinette, examining some little china figurines while Lady Royce pulled the elaborate draperies back from the windows. None of them were wearing blue.

Oh, really! she thought, with a little irritated tap of her foot. If there *was* a ghost in here, she wanted very much to see it. Why would it keep running away?

Then she looked back to the portrait, to the man who looked so much like the doubting Lord Royce.

Maybe Louisa had a good reason for hiding after all, if her husband had been half as pigheaded as this Lord Royce. She probably felt one lifetime tolerating him was quite enough.

"Yes, Louisa *did* have a sad history," Lady Royce sighed, tying back the last of the draperies with their gold cords. "So very lonely, out here all alone."

There was a small sound that echoed in the air like an irritated huff.

"I am surprised she would wish to stay here, then, at the site of her unhappiness," Chat commented uncertainly. "I certainly would wish to move on."

Cassie smiled at her aunt. Chat did not always believe all this business about ghosts, but at least she tried. She did not scoff and make fun, like *some* people.

Antoinette, who stood beside the bed with one hand on the satin hangings, said, "Perhaps she cannot move on. Perhaps the sad events of her life keep her here. But she is not sad now. And she is interested in our activities."

"She is here, then? In this room?" Lady Royce asked eagerly.

"Oh, yes. Most assuredly." Antoinette closed her eyes and placed her fingertips lightly at her temples. "But she is not sure about showing herself yet. She doesn't wish to be misunderstood, as she was in her life."

The others crowded in closer around her.

"What was misunderstood about her?" Lady Royce whispered.

Antoinette shook her head. "I do not know. My powers are limited without my books and guides, unlike my mother, who could see things very clearly. And the daylight is too harsh."

"But I want to know!" Lady Royce cried. "I *want* to understand her."

Cassie quite agreed. They only wanted to talk to Louisa, to understand her. And anyone else who might be about.

She thought Louisa was behaving like a little brat.

Antoinette touched Lady Royce's arm reassuringly. "We will soon find out. If you like, we can come back here at night, with my mother's book of incantations. We will discover more then."

Lady Royce and Cassie enthusiastically agreed, even though Chat still looked doubtful. As they left the East Tower and walked back to the inhabited sections of the castle, Antoinette said, "Tell me about Lady Lettice, Lady Royce. The one who has not been seen here of late."

"I fear I do not know much about her," Lady Royce said in a regretful tone. "She has not been seen since my husband's parents' time. She was the daughter of the earl, and served as a maid of honor to Queen Elizabeth. She never married or had children. I do not know why she would come back here after her death, or why she would leave."

"Hmm," Antoinette said, tapping her finger thoughtfully on her chin.

"Do you sense *her* presence?" Cassie asked.

"Not now," Antoinette answered. "But perhaps later . . ."

"Oh, there you are," a voice interrupted as they walked past the open door of the library. Lord Royce emerged from the dim depths of the room, like Merlin exiting his cave, and gave them all a polite smile. "You were certainly on your tour a long while."

"There is much to see in the castle, dear," his mother said. "As you would know, if you did not spend all your time in just this one room."

He laughed. "Well, Mother, you will be glad to know I am going to remedy that. I was just going down to the stables, and wanted to see if Miss Richards would care to accompany me, now that your tour is finished." He turned his lingering smile onto Cassie.

Cassie examined him carefully, his smile and his coolly polite eyes. So, the Doubting Thomas wanted to be hospitable now, did he?

Well, no one could accuse Cassandra Richards of forgetting the lessons her mother had taught her about not being a rude houseguest. She nodded and gave him a smile of her own.

"Thank you, Lord Royce," she said. "I would be happy to come."

Chapter Eight

Cassie followed Lord Royce down the pathway that led to the stables. He was very quiet on their walk, and so was she; she wasn't exactly sure what to say to him.

She wondered if he felt like his mother was forcing him into taking her riding, and it made her feel rather awkward.

Awkwardness had been an unaccustomed feeling until she came here. At home, in Jamaica, she had had her share of admirers. Her dance card was always full, and she never seemed to lack for conversation. And even at Aunt Chat's house in Bath, where she often felt shy and strange, she enjoyed the company of the card parties and concerts.

Why did she always feel so tongue-tied and awkward around Lord Royce in particular? He was just a scoffing scholar.

Albeit a handsome one.

Then they turned a bend in the path, and she lost any awkward feeling at the surprise of the beautiful view.

They were at a lower level here than they were at

the castle, nearer to the sea. A low stone wall lined the edge of the pathway, where it veered closer to the cliff. Cassie went to lean on the crumbling stone, wide-eyed, as she looked at the vista.

From the castle, the sea was undeniably lovely, but here it was more elemental. She could hear the rush of the waves as they hit the pebbly shore and then receded.

"Beautiful, isn't it?" Lord Royce said, coming to stand beside her at the wall.

Cassie smiled up at him, bringing her hand up to shield her eyes from the afternoon sun. "Very beautiful," she answered. At least *that* they could agree on.

"You sound rather surprised," he said amiably, propping his hip against the wall so that he was half-turned to face her. "I don't spend all my time immured in the library, you know. I do get out once in a while to breathe fresh air."

"And go riding along the cliffs," Cassie murmured. She remembered her vision of him from this morning, galloping along like a wild pirate.

"Yes. Of course." He turned his gaze away from her, back to the sea. "Miss Richards, my mother looks very sweet and harmless, but she can be quite ruthless when she wants something. And she is not above using someone's politeness as a guest to further her own ends. If you really *don't* want to go riding with me, I will understand. We could tell her you did not find a horse to your liking. I am sure you would prefer to be looking for your ghosts rather than spending time with me."

Cassie turned to him, surprised. "Oh, no! I *would* like to go riding with you. Unless . . ." Her voice faltered as a thought struck her. Was he trying to get rid of her? "Unless you have work you must be doing. I would hate to keep you from it."

He gave her a startlingly charming smile. "Nonsense. No one in their right mind would rather be inside working than out in the sunshine with such a lovely companion. The Peloponnesian War can wait until later."

She smiled at him tentatively in return. "Why, Lord Royce. Was that a compliment?"

He laughed. "Shocking, I know. But, despite what my mother may think, I am not completely socially inept. I can pay compliments as well as the next gentleman, when they are sincere."

"*I* never thought you were socially inept," Cassie said, almost truthfully. Emboldened by his new, more comfortable presence, she said, "Do you know what I would really like to do today?"

"No, Miss Richards. Look for spirits, mayhap?"

Cassie peered at him suspiciously, but his smile was only teasing, not mocking. "I would like to take a walk down by the shore."

"Really? Well, that is easily done. The stables will always wait. But I fear it is rather chilly down by the water."

Cassie held out a handful of her heavy red cloak. "Oh, I am always prepared for the chill here!"

"Then there are some steps just a little further down that way, that lead to the shore." He straightened from leaning on the wall, and offered her his arm. "Shall we, Miss Richards?"

Cassie eyed his proffered arm for a moment, half-afraid he might pull away and laugh at her. But when he just held it out a little farther and smiled at her expectantly, she slowly slid her hand into the warm crook of his elbow and let him lead her onward.

The steps to the shore, made of stone at the lowest part of the cliffs, were steep and weathered. Cassie

moved carefully on the thin soles of her half boots,
but Lord Royce's arm beneath her hand was steady
and strong as he helped her down.

Surely he did not spend *all* his time in the library,
or the muscles that bunched and moved under her
touch would not be so—so *hard*.

Finally she was distracted from her very improper
thoughts about Lord Royce's musculature when they
reached the shore, and her face was sprayed with a
light mist from the sea. She inhaled deeply of the
salty tang in the air, so strange but so familiar and
sweet. Her footsteps crunched on the pebbles of the
beach.

She could not help herself. She let go of Lord
Royce's arm and rushed toward the water, until the
waves lapped at the very toes of her half boots and
dampened the hems of her dress and cloak.

Cassie did not even notice. She was far too en-
thralled with being so close to the sea again. She gave
a little laugh and knelt down to trail her fingertips
in a receding wave. The water was much colder than
in Jamaica, but it felt delicious on her skin.

She stood back up and glanced over her shoulder
at Lord Royce. She expected to find him disapproving of her impulsive behavior, perhaps ready to de-
mand that they return to the castle at once. She was
all ready to stiffen her resolve not to let him spoil
her joy.

Instead, she found that he watched her almost as
if he had never seen her before in his life. His expression was quite startled, his eyes wide. He was frowning a bit, but not in a disapproving way. Rather, he
looked—puzzled.

Cassie was not sure what to make of this. She
moved one small step closer to him. "The sea is very
beautiful, is it not?" she said slowly.

"Oh, yes," he answered in a quiet voice, the sound almost lost in the murmur of the waves. "Very beautiful."

Phillip watched Cassie run toward the water, her laughter echoing on the autumn air, and thought that she looked a bit like a clothed Aphrodite, emerging newborn from the waves. If Aphrodite had chosen chilly Cornwall to emerge from instead of the warm Mediterranean at Sicily, of course.

At the castle, Cassie seemed happy and sociable, but also strangely uncomfortable at times. Almost as if she was afraid of saying or doing something that was in some way wrong. Here there was none of that in her demeanor. She ran toward the water, laughing, her hand stretched out.

As she bent down to touch a receding wave, a lock of black hair fell from her carved ebony combs and brushed against her cheek.

She looked so—so *joyful*. Phillip longed to join her, to feel that way again. To feel free, childlike, to not worry about books and logic and always being in strictest control. He wanted to absorb all her laughter and wonder into himself.

Even to believe in spirits and fairies, perhaps?

Then she looked back at him with her rich, dark eyes. "The sea is beautiful, is it not?" she said, looking at him with a rather puzzled air.

"Oh, yes," he murmured hoarsely. "Very beautiful."

Her eyes widened, as if startled, and he suddenly realized he was gaping at her like a moonstruck schoolboy. A small frown formed on her brow, and his longings of only a moment before vanished like so much mist on the water. He was recalled to himself, to where they were, to *who* they were.

"There are underground tunnels near here," he said, grasping for something, anything, to talk about. Anything that did not involve how lovely her eyes were. "They are said to have been used by pirates long ago, but they are mostly blocked up now to discourage smuggling. Except for one."

"Pirates! How very intriguing," she said. She looked away from him, breaking the last vestiges of the strange spell. "I should like to see them."

"There is not much to see. The one that is still open is just used for storage. Local fishermen keep their boats there."

"I should still like to see it, and imagine the pirates that used to shelter there. I am sure Aunt Chat and Antoinette would like to see it, too."

"Maybe we could all have a picnic near there, one day soon," Phillip said. He found himself grasping at the excuse to spend more time with this strange, intriguing woman. Even leaving his books yet again for a picnic by the sea.

She smiled at him, quite as if they were almost friends. "Yes. I would enjoy that very much. *We* would enjoy that."

Chapter Nine

Cassie was awakened in the middle of the night by the unmistakable tingling sensation of someone staring at her. She opened her eyes—and promptly gave a shriek. Quick as a flash, she scrambled up against the pillows.

"Hello," said the woman who perched on the edge of the bed. "I am sorry I frightened you."

Cassie pulled the sheet up to her chin and stared over it at the woman. She appeared quite solid: a real person, with long blond ringlets and a blue satin gown in the style of the Restoration. Only a faint, white glow around the edges betrayed her as something not *quite* human.

Cassie recognized her face from the portraits. "You—you are Louisa, aren't you?" she managed to stammer out. She wasn't exactly sure how one should address a ghost. Should she have called her Lady Royce?

But Louisa didn't seem to mind the informality of being addressed by her given name. She just nodded, and lounged back on her elbow. "I am! I saw all of you in my tower today and thought I ought to introduce myself. I truly did not mean to scare you."

Cassie lowered the sheet slowly. "You did not scare me. I was simply startled. It is not every day a ghost comes and sits on my bed."

Louisa laughed, a rather strange, echoing sound. "Then I did not mean to *startle* you. I just wanted to talk."

"Then you don't mind that we were in your tower?"

"Mind? Certainly not. It makes a nice change from having only old Sir Belvedere to talk to."

Cassie relaxed back against the pillows. It was beginning to feel almost *normal* to converse with a slightly glowing, long-dead person. "Who is Sir Belvedere?"

"He lives here, too. He was a knight who served the first Earl of Royce, in the fourteenth century. He was killed when the castle was being built, so he has been here for a *very* long time. Much longer than me."

"Killed? How?"

"He tripped on some building materials and fell from the tower. He never talks about it, not in all the years I have known him. He was wearing his silly armor at the time. Truth to tell, he can be a bit of a bore, but he is better company than none. It has been rather quiet around here for a long time."

There was a clanking noise from the corridor. Cassie startled and looked toward the door. "What was that?"

"Oh, that was just Sir Belvedere. He is hovering about in the corridor. He thinks it is improper for him to enter a lady's chamber, but he is just as curious as I am."

There was another clanking sound.

"If he does not cease doing that, he will wake the whole household," Louisa said, but she did not really seem terribly concerned by the prospect.

"Perhaps I could meet him later," Cassie said hopefully. She thought it would be quite interesting to see a ghost in armor.

Louisa gave her a secretive little smile. "Perhaps."

"Is he the only other ghost in residence here?"

"At the moment, yes. There have been others, but they come and go. The only other people who have stayed as long as Sir Belvedere and myself were Lady Lettice and Angelo. We have not seen them for several years, though, so we think they must have moved across."

"Moved across?"

"That is when the ghosts leave to go on to the next plane, a place I have not seen yet. I don't know why some of us get trapped here and some move on right away. It's a mystery."

"But if there are so many of you, why do the people living in the castle never see you?"

"Oh, they do sometimes!" She laughed lightly. "You see, though, there is one great advantage to being a ghost, once you learn the trick of it, and that is that we can be visible or invisible as we choose. Just as I choose to be visible to you right now."

Cassie thought that must be quite an advantage. "And you choose to be *invisible* to Lord Royce?"

Louisa shrugged. "It makes it more fun that way."

"So you and this Sir Belvedere have been the only ones here for a long time, except for Lady Lettice and this—Angelo?" Cassie had heard about Lady Lettice, but never of any Angelo. "Who is, or was, he?"

Before Louisa could answer, the door connecting Cassie's room to Antoinette's opened, and Antoinette stood there, holding a candle and a bunch of herbs. She looked every bit the Yaumumi priestess her mother had been, in a flowing red dressing gown, with her thick, waving black hair falling over her shoulders.

"I thought I heard voices." She held up the bundle in her hand, eyeing Louisa carefully. "I brought herbs, in case there were evil spirits to be sent away. But I see they won't be needed."

Louisa laughed, obviously quite pleased to be suspected of being an evil spirit.

"Indeed not," Cassie said. "Louisa isn't the least bit evil. Come and meet her. She has been telling me the most interesting things."

Antoinette tucked the herbs away in the pocket of her robe and hurried over to sit down on the bed across from Louisa. She placed her candle on the bedside table, and its golden glow made Louisa appear slightly more transparent.

"How do you do," said Antoinette.

"So you are the one with all the spells and potions," Louisa said, her eyes wide with wonder. "Sir Belvedere thinks you might be able to find what became of Lady Lettice for us."

There was more clanking and knocking from the corridor.

"That is Sir Belvedere," Cassie explained. "He thinks it is improper for him to come in here."

"Very polite of him," Antoinette answered. She tapped one long finger thoughtfully on her chin. "I could certainly *try* to summon up Lady Lettice for you, if you would like to see her again. It would be an interesting challenge."

Louisa leaned forward eagerly. "Sir Belvedere and I would help you. Oh, it would be so *nice* to have some excitement here again! I end up playing chess in the East Tower with Sir Belvedere every night, and he cheats horribly."

"Vile slander!" a voice cried in the corridor.

"It is an incantation I have never tried before," Antoinette warned.

"But I have every faith in your powers, dear Antoinette," Cassie said with a thrill of excitement and apprehension at the thought of a new incantation.

"We would have to try it this Friday, when the moon is in the right phase."

"Could we invite Lady Royce and Aunt Chat?" Cassie said. "I am sure they would not want to miss it."

Antoinette gave her a sly little smile. "And Lord Royce, too? Perhaps we could make a believer of him."

Louisa snorted in a most unladylike fashion. "Nay, not him! He is too much like my own husband. Cynical and doubting. William never saw the truth of what was before him, either." She looked away, but before she did, Cassie saw her glowing blue eyes turn sad.

"I think we *should* invite him," Cassie said. "It might be quite interesting to have him there." She laughed, but she could not forget that flash of sadness in Louisa's eyes. Cassie wondered how *she* would feel if her own husband did not understand her. But then she shook her head. That would never happen, since she had no plans to ever take a husband!

"Very well," said Antoinette. "We shall make a party of it, then. This Friday, in the East Tower, I think. We will make a believer of Lord Royce if it is the last thing we do."

Chapter Ten

"I think we should have a ball," Lady Royce announced the next morning as they all walked along the cliffs on their way to a picnic.

"A ball, Mother?" Lord Royce said, shifting the large hamper under his arm. "Who would we invite?"

"Why, all the neighbors, of course! They are all back from Town, and from their holidays in Brighton and Bath, and they haven't been invited to the castle in a very long time. We should do *something* to entertain our guests properly."

"Oh, don't go to any trouble on our account, Melinda," said Chat. "We are quite happy just being here. Are we not, girls?"

Cassie and Antoinette murmured in agreement, but secretly Cassie thought a ball sounded splendid.

"Nonsense!" Lady Royce cried. "We will have a ball. A masked ball! There is a dressmaker in the village who can do our costumes for us. I will have her come to the castle this week!" It was obvious that she had thought about this ball idea quite a bit.

"A masked ball?" Lord Royce said, his handsome face the picture of dismay.

"Yes! A masked ball. You can wear a toga, dear, or whatever it was Greeks wore. You don't need to worry about a thing, Phillip. I will plan it all." Then Lady Royce took Chat's arm and led her ahead on the pathway, saying, "Now, Chat dear, you do so much entertaining in Bath, I would like your opinion on the menu for the ball . . ."

Antoinette walked ahead with them, leaving Cassie alone with Lord Royce. They followed the three women slowly.

"You do not seem very enthusiastic about the idea of a ball, Lord Royce," Cassie said.

"It would be very—interesting. You can tell a great deal about people by what they choose to dress as at a masked ball," he answered, but his expression was still doubtful.

"Indeed." Then, since she was rather excited by the idea of the dance and didn't want him dampening her enthusiasm, she changed the topic. "My aunt tells us that your work on ancient Greece is very well known. I've already told you that you are quite admired by the members of her Philosophical Society."

He tilted his head as he looked at her, as if puzzled by her words. "I have had some modest success," he said quietly. "Though some say it is not proper for an earl to write and publish, I feel that the knowledge is too important not to share, no matter what the gossip."

"Quite right. And how is it you became so interested in Greece?"

"Do you truly wish to know, Miss Richards?" he asked, taking her elbow in his free hand to help her down the steps to the shore. Even through the thick wool of her pelisse, his touch was warm and reassuring. "Or are you just being polite?"

Cassie would never have thought she would truly

be interested in the intricacies of ancient Greece. But she found that, strangely enough, she was. Very much. "I am interested."

"When I was a child, my father had a book about the wonders of ancient Greece. I read it over and over until it fell apart. It inspired me to study the classics at Oxford," he said. "But other than that one book, I did not know much about the ancient world. My tutors, and the school I attended, were much more concerned with the running of estates and playing cricket. It was at Oxford that I first read Socrates and Plato and Aristotle, and they opened my eyes to so many things."

"Things such as what?" Cassie asked, intrigued.

"Well, for a beginning, they emphasized logic and the meanings of words. They based their beliefs on empirical knowledge rather than religion or rituals or myth. They sought natural explanations for natural phenomena. Our own world seems so very chaotic at times, do you not agree? With the wars, and Prinny in charge, and all these poets running about."

"Hmm," Cassie answered slowly, going over his words in her mind. "Order *can* be comforting. It was a great relief to me to be in Aunt Chat's safe, comfortable home after the confusion of my father's death. But the Greeks were not always so reasonable, were they? I mean, the Delphic Oracle was not such a sensible idea, was it, yet they believed it. And they had plenty of poets of their own 'running about.' "

She expected him to quarrel with her, and stiffened her shoulders in preparation to retort. After all, it was rather intimidating to argue with a scholar when one knew almost nothing about the subject.

But, to her surprise, Lord Royce just laughed, and said, "Touché, Miss Richards! And quite right, too.

There are some things about human nature that never change. I should know that, from all the reading I have done of late on the foolishness of the Greek wars."

"Exactly so. The horrors of war do not change. Neither does family, or honor, or—or love."

Lord Royce looked at her, and, for one long, sweet moment, Cassie felt that they were in accord with one another. She wanted so much to go on talking of these things, things she had never really stopped to think about before, but Lady Royce called out to them.

"Come along, you two!" she cried over the sound of the waves. "What are you dawdling about for? We have found the perfect place for our picnic, here behind these rocks."

Lord Royce smiled at Cassie, and led the way over to where the others were waiting. Chat had already spread the blanket out carefully on the sand, and they waited only for the hamper Lord Royce carried.

It *was* the perfect place, Cassie thought as she settled herself on the blanket next to Antoinette and leaned back against a large rock. The crash of the waves was muffled here, and the wind turned away. She would *almost* have thought herself warm, with the pale sunlight beaming down on her uncovered head. It held all the promise of a perfect afternoon, with good friends and the sea.

Yet she almost wished she was alone with Lord Royce, so they could just go on and on talking, with him watching her with his lovely gray eyes.

"What were you two speaking of?" Lady Royce asked, unpacking the bounty of pork pies, cold chicken, and apple tarts from the hamper. "You were talking so *intently*."

"Your son was telling me about his work, Lady

Royce," Cassie said. "About the philosophy of ancient Greece."

"You poor dear! Here, you must be in need of some sherry." Lady Royce poured out a generous measure of the dark gold liquid and passed it over the hamper to Cassie.

"Mother! I am hardly in the habit of boring guests so deeply that they require potent drinks to stay conscious," Lord Royce muttered.

Cassie laughed and sipped her sherry. "Indeed, I was not bored, Lady Royce! I found it quite fascinating."

"After the exciting life you must have lived in the Indies?" Lady Royce sounded most disbelieving.

"Jamaica was not always as exciting as all that," Cassie said, thinking back on the long, hot, lazy days, and the flower-scented nights, when the distant sounds of drums and the ocean would come through her open window.

No, not terribly exciting. But very sweet.

"Not exciting at all?" Lady Royce said in a disappointed voice.

"Well, there *were* a lot of parties. Especially when my mother was alive. How she loved to dance!" Cassie smiled at the memory.

"My brother's wife was a beautiful woman," Chat offered. "And a vivacious spirit."

"Indeed? What of *your* mother, Miss Duvall? Was she also a—vivacious spirit?" Lady Royce asked Antoinette.

"My mother was devoted to her studies, Lady Royce," Antoinette answered. "Just as your son is."

"People came from all over the island to hear her wisdom," said Cassie.

"Just like the Delphic Oracle," Lord Royce murmured. "I should very much like to hear about it sometime."

"Would you truly? Or are you just being polite?" Cassie teased, echoing his earlier words to her.

He laughed. "I assure you, Miss Richards, I am never 'just polite.'"

After they finished eating, Cassie, Antoinette, and Lord Royce set off to look at the tunnels, leaving Chat and Lady Royce to their gossip and the last of the sherry.

The passages were mostly blocked up, just as Lord Royce had said they would be, and what was left was drafty and damp. Sand and pebbles had blown in to form a thin layer on the hard-packed floor. There were crates piled up along the cold walls, and a few upturned fishing boats.

Cassie thought, with a small thrill, that it looked like a smuggler's lair. She leaned back against one of the boats and looked around, wondering what sort of daring adventures had once happened in these tunnels.

Suddenly, her reverie was broken when Antoinette gave a scream and collapsed into a heap on the dirty floor. Her green cloak spread about her in a dark pool.

"Antoinette!" Cassie cried, running across the tunnel to fall down on her knees at her friend's side. "Antoinette, what is it?" She placed Antoinette's head carefully on her lap and rubbed at her cold wrists, wishing desperately that she was the sort to carry smelling salts around with her.

"What happened?" Lord Royce said, his voice hoarse with concern, as he knelt down beside them. "Is Miss Duvall ill?"

"She was perfectly well before," Cassie answered, frantically waving her hand in front of Antoinette's face. "Perhaps it was something she ate!"

"But we all ate the same things. Do *you* feel ill, Miss Richards?"

"Not a bit. Oh, Antoinette, do wake up, please!"

As if in answer to Cassie's panicked entreaties, Antoinette's ebony eyes fluttered open, and she glanced quickly about. "Cassie? What has happened?"

"Thank heaven you are conscious!" Cassie said in great relief. "You fainted."

"Did I? How very odd." She struggled to sit up, with Cassie and Lord Royce's help. Her turban was askew, and she pressed her palm to her forehead as if in pain. "I would like some water, please, if there is any."

"I will just fetch it, then," said Lord Royce. "Miss Richards, you stay here with Miss Duvall and lower her head to her knees if she feels faint again. I will not be gone long." Then he hurried off on his errand.

As soon as he was gone, Antoinette clutched at Cassie's hand and whispered, "We must come *here* on Friday night, not the East Tower. I feel that Lady Lettice's presence is very strong here."

"Is that why you fainted?" Cassie whispered back. "You sense something frightening here?"

Antoinette shook her head slowly. "Not frightening. Just—strong. We must come back here."

"Of course we will come back. On Friday. But you mustn't worry about it now. Are you feeling better?"

"Oh, yes, quite. I must have just been overwhelmed. Here, help me to stand, and we will wait for Lord Royce outside."

"How is Miss Duvall feeling, Miss Richards?"

Cassie, who was hurrying past the open door of the library with a basin of lavender water in her hands, paused to peer into the dimly lit room. Phillip came to stand in the doorway, his gray gaze inscrutable behind his spectacles.

"Much better, thank you, Lord Royce," Cassie answered, thinking how odd it was that he should care. All the men in Jamaica, and even in Bath, had seen Antoinette as nothing but a servant and an oddity. They would never have inquired after her health.

But Phillip appeared truly concerned.

"I was just taking this to her," Cassie added, holding up the basin. "Lavender water is very good for headaches."

"Does Miss Duvall care for wine?" he asked. "I have some very nice German wine put away in the cellar. I could send it up to her."

"How kind of you!" Cassie said with a smile. "So thoughtful . . ."

Phillip waved away her thanks with an awkward gesture. "Not at all, Miss Richards. I am only sorry that your day, and Miss Duvall's, was marred by illness."

"Yes. It was such a lovely day."

He nodded. "Lovely," he murmured. Then, looking rather abashed by that one word he had spoken, he backed up into the library. "I will send that wine up to Miss Duvall. Please let me know if there is anything else I can do."

"Thank you, Lord Royce." Cassie went on her way with her basin, thoroughly bemused by the mystifying Lord Royce. It seemed like every day she found that there was much more to him than books and studies and logic.

Chapter Eleven

"Don't they make a charming picture?" Lady Royce said, looking up from her embroidery to smile fondly across the drawing room at her son and Cassandra.

Antoinette had retired after supper with a lingering headache, but the others had gathered in the drawing room. Phillip and Cassandra were seated together at the pianoforte, attempting a duet. Unfortunately, neither of them was particularly musical, and the discordant plonking noise echoed in the large room.

Chat winced at an especially strident note, and laid down another card in her game of Patience. "Charming. But do you suppose they could engage in something *quiet*, like cards? Or reading?"

"Then we could not admire your niece's talent at the pianoforte!" Lady Royce protested. "Every young lady should play a musical instrument, do you not agree, Chat?"

"Almost every young lady," Chat murmured. She had to agree that Cassie looked very pretty bent over the ivory keys, her dark pink silk skirts spread about her. Chat only hoped that, with all the ghosts floating about the castle, Mozart did not choose to join them, full of wrath at the mangling of his concerto.

"Miss Richards is a very pretty girl indeed," Lady Royce continued. "I must confess I had no idea what to expect, since she had spent so long away from England."

Chat gave a little smile and laid down another card. "Did you think she would wear grass skirts or some such, Melinda?"

Lady Royce blushed, ducking her head over her sewing. "Of course not! I just—wasn't sure."

"Yes. Her parents were not precisely conventional, not like my older brother the viscount. I am not sure Cassandra would pass muster with the high sticklers at Almack's! But she has her own charms."

"Oh, assuredly! She is very pretty, as I said. And obviously kindhearted." Lady Royce gave Chat a sly smile. "Phillip seems to like her a great deal."

Chat looked back over at the young couple. They appeared to be quarreling over a piece of sheet music, with Cassie attempting to pull it out of his hands. "Oh, yes," she said wryly. "You can tell how much they like each other just by looking at them."

"She seems just the sort who could make him come out of his library and into the world. He never would have left his books to go on a picnic before Miss Richards came here, let alone agree to a masked ball!" Lady Royce nodded decisively. "Yes, she is *very* good for him."

But would *he* be good for *her*, Chat wondered. He did have a title and a tidy fortune. But Cassie had her own fortune and was such a free spirit. Could someone like Lord Royce make her happy?

Chat's own comfortable marriage to Lord Willowby, which had lasted twenty harmonious years before his death, made her want nothing less for her niece. A title could not make deep incompatibilities just disappear.

Still, she had to admit that they did look very handsome together.

"You are playing it all wrong!" Cassie said, taking the piece of now rather tattered music from Lord Royce's hand and putting it on the stand. "See these notes here and here? All wrong!"

"My dear Miss Richards, *I* am not the one who is tone-deaf," he muttered.

Cassie stared at him. "Look at the tin ear calling *me* tone-deaf! I thought earls were supposed to be gallant, or at the very least polite."

"Very well! I am very sorry, Miss Richards. Please forgive me for my rudeness. Why don't you play the solo part, and I will turn the pages?"

Cassie looked from him to the music doubtfully. The truth was, she *was* a bit tone-deaf, and had always detested the music lessons her father made her take. Only politeness to Lady Royce, who had asked her to play for them, had made her sit down at the pianoforte. She had not thought Lord Royce would join her there, and now her self-consciousness was making her rather testy.

She gave him an apologetic little smile and said, "I do not really feel like playing anymore. Perhaps *you* would favor us with a song, and I will just go and sit down by the fire for a while."

"As you wish, Miss Richards," he answered. "But I really do apologize for what I said. I am sure you are truly a masterful musician."

"Apology accepted," she said with a laugh. "But flattery denied. I am really a horrible musician."

"That cannot be true."

Oh, but it *was* true. And what was worse, Cassie

found as she went to sit down beside Lady Royce,
Lord Royce was quite a competent musician. Not a
Mozart, by any means, but tuneful and regular. Only
trying to keep up with her had made him play in
the wrong key.

She had to laugh inwardly at herself, for always
behaving like such a silly goose around him.

"Your aunt and I were just talking about what
your life must have been like before you came to
England, my dear Miss Richards," Lady Royce said.
"How interesting it must have been in Jamaica! And
how very different from here."

That was certainly undeniable. "It is rather different,
yes."

"But you did say that your parents gave a great
many entertainments. There must have been some
society there."

"There were the families from the neighboring plantations,
like Mr. Bates and his sister, and the Smith-
Thompkins, and several people who lived in Negril.
They came quite often to our house, and we went into
town frequently. After Mother died, Father and I kept
to ourselves more, but we still went to card parties
and musicales, and even the occasional ball. No, there
was no lack of society in Jamaica, Lady Royce."

"You must have had a good many suitors, too,"
Lady Royce said, pretending great absorption in
her embroidery.

"A few," Cassie answered, thinking especially of
the persistent Mr. Bates, who had come to the docks
to propose one last time before she left.

He had certainly been very different from Lord
Royce, loud and boastful. He had probably never
opened a book in his life.

"But you accepted none of them?" Lady Royce
persisted.

"I did not care for any of them in that way."

"Oh, yes, I see." Lady Royce chuckled. "Yes, I *do* see."

Chat laughed.

Cassie wondered what they were up to, but she was just too tired to puzzle it out at present. "I think I will just go check on Antoinette before I retire, if you will excuse me."

"Oh, yes, dear, do," said Chat. "Make sure she has drunk the brandy and warm milk we sent up."

"I will. Good night, Aunt Chat, Lady Royce." Cassie kissed her aunt's cheek, and left the drawing room with the strains of Mozart floating behind her.

Antoinette was not alone in her chamber. Sitting across from her at a small table, playing what appeared to be a game of Beggar My Neighbor, was Louisa. She was wearing a cloak tonight, a puffy blue satin affair, with the hood pushed back and her golden ringlets spilling free.

"There you are," said Antoinette, studying the cards in her hand. "We've been waiting for you."

Cassie went and sat down in the empty chair at the table. "Have you? For what?"

"I thought you might like to meet Sir Belvedere tonight." Louisa laid down another card and crowed, "I win again! I suppose my card-playing skills are not so dormant as I thought."

Antoinette shook her head. "It is not fair! You have had almost two hundred years to practice."

"You've had practice, too, Antoinette," said Cassie. "We did nothing but play cards all those weeks on the ship from Jamaica. Now, tell me, is Sir Belvedere coming here to meet us?"

"Oh, no," answered Louisa. "He still thinks it is

improper to come to a living lady's chamber. We will
go to the East Tower."

"When? Now?"

"Of course, if you are ready." Louisa pulled her
hood up over her head, and glided toward the door.
"Just follow me!"

Then she disappeared through the solid door, leaving only a faint shimmer behind her.

"We can scarcely follow you that way, now, can
we?" Antoinette called, standing up and reaching
with her stockinged feet for the slippers she had
discarded.

A merry laugh echoed, and Louisa stuck her head
back through the door. "So sorry, my dears! Just a
bit of ghost humor. Sometimes I simply cannot
help myself."

The East Tower was dark and chilly, since the
maids did not go there to light fires or adjust the
draperies. Only Antoinette's and Cassie's candles cast
light into the shadows of the corners.

Louisa settled herself in a chair next to the window
and called out, "Sir Belvedere! Where are you? You
have callers. I hope you have polished your armor
up for them."

There was a faint clattering noise, which grew
louder and louder as they listened. Cassie could not
tell where the sound was coming from, even though
she twisted her head this way and that, peering into
the gloom. Then there was one last, deafening clank,
and a tall figure in armor appeared next to Louisa's
chair.

He pushed the visor back on his helmet, and Cassie saw that he was a rather handsome, if very
pale, gentleman.

"Fair ladies!" he cried, giving them a noisy, stiff

little bow. "I am honored you came all this way to make my humble acquaintance."

Cassie glanced at Antoinette, but her friend appeared to be as much at a loss as she was. What did one do with a ghost knight? Curtsy? Shake hands?

She was every bit as puzzled as she had been when she first met Louisa.

She ended up giving a small bob and saying, "How do you do? I am Miss Cassandra Richards, and this is Miss Antoinette Duvall."

"Miss Duvall is going to find Lady Lettice for us," Louisa said.

"Indeed! I have heard you have great powers, Miss Duvall," said Sir Belvedere, holding up his slipping visor to look at Antoinette. "Very great."

Antoinette demurred. "Not *very* great. Not at all like my mother. But I will help you in any way I can. And I know that we would very much like to hear *your* story, Sir Belvedere."

"Ah, my tale. 'Tis a sad one." Sir Belvedere sighed and lowered himself into the chair next to Louisa's. His legs stuck out stiffly in front of him.

Louisa twisted one of her ringlets around her finger. "It is not as sad as all that. Not nearly as sad as *my* story."

Sir Belvedere gave an indignant huff. "Getting drunk and falling down the cliff is not *sad*."

"Neither is tripping on a loose stone and falling off the tower into the moat," Louisa retorted.

Cassie watched them bickering, and wondered if there was something in the air of Royce Castle that caused silly arguments, like the one she and Lord Royce had had over the music.

Then again, did ghosts even breathe air? She had no idea.

And it appeared that this was a long-standing conversation between Louisa and Sir Belvedere. They just shook their heads and looked away from each other to smile at Cassie and Antoinette.

Antoinette perched herself on the edge of the high bed. "I don't remember seeing a moat here," she said.

"It was filled in after Louisa's time," Sir Belvedere explained.

"My husband's brother's wife, who was Lady Royce after me, thought it smelled too foul," Louisa sniffed. "I rather miss it, though."

Cassie sat down on the bed next to Antoinette, listening as Sir Belvedere went on to tell some tales of life at Royce Castle in the Middle Ages, and marveling at the entire strange scene. She had grown up surrounded by tales of spells and spirits, and had never doubted the existence of an unseen world. But she had never thought she would be sitting about casually conversing with two ghosts.

And she would never have thought it would be so very *ordinary*. They chatted about all the other generations Sir Belvedere and Louisa had seen come and go, the ghosts that had stayed for a while and then gone on to nobody knew where. They talked of Cassie's and Antoinette's lives in Jamaica, about Antoinette's mother and Cassie's parents.

It really could have been any tea party anywhere, if their fellow conversants had not been slightly glowing about the edges.

Then the talk turned to the current living inhabitants of Royce Castle.

"We quite like Lady Royce, don't we, Sir Belvedere?" Louisa said. "She's always trying to talk to us."

"A fine lady indeed. Much better than her mother-in-law ever was," Sir Belvedere agreed. "You would have thought that a lady whose marriage was arranged by Lady Lettice would be more receptive to spirits, but no."

"But Lady Royce's son is very different. Always so *logical*," said Louisa. She made "logical" sound like a rather dirty little word. "Always buried in a book. But he is fun to tease a bit."

"We switch his papers about all the time," Sir Belvedere added. "He just thinks it is the housemaids, and asks his mother not to let them tidy in there anymore."

Louisa laughed. "He always forgets that no one *does* clean in there! They stopped months ago." Then she turned a shrewd look onto Cassie. "I think Miss Richards rather *likes* Lord Royce, though."

"Does she indeed?" Sir Belvedere said in a highly interested tone.

"She thinks he looks like a dashing poet," Antoinette offered.

"*Antoinette!*" Cassie cried, feeling her face grow warm. She pressed her palms to her cheeks. "Please."

"Well, do you not think that?" Antoinette said innocently.

"We could assist you," said Sir Belvedere. "Put some suggestions into his head, that sort of thing."

"Oh, no! Thank you, but no," Cassie said hurriedly. That was the very last thing she needed; ghosts matchmaking for her.

Antoinette then said, "He is not really her 'sort of gentleman,' you see."

And, without explaining who she *did* think of as her sort of gentleman, Cassie said good night and retired back to her own chamber.

Chapter Twelve

Once in her bed, though, Cassie found she simply could not sleep. The excitement of talking to the ghosts still hummed in her mind, and she tossed about for a long while remembering it.

Finally, she gave up any attempt to fall asleep, pushed back the bedclothes, found her slippers and dressing gown, and went downstairs to the library.

There she bypassed the shelf of novels and found the neat row of leather-bound books that bore Lord Royce's name on the spines. She pulled out the first volume and took it over to the desk.

She sat in the thick silence of the night. Time stood still as she turned over the pages of the book. She wasn't sure what she had expected when she opened the volume, but not this complete absorption into another world.

She had thought Lord Royce's work would be dry and academic, and it was certainly very learned. But it was also warm and vivid; it brought scenes of an ancient, long-dead place to life. She could almost see the public squares of Greece, where philosophers taught rapt young students and servants hurried to the marketplace bearing amphorae of olives and wine. It almost made her think of Jamaica.

Cassie did not see the logic that Lord Royce claimed to hold so dear, but she did see much more. And she also saw that Lord Royce saw more, too. Probably more than even he realized. He saw the true vividness of life. Why, then, would he deny the richness of what was in his own home?

Cassie was very puzzled. Both by Lord Royce and by herself.

Then, as she eagerly turned over another page, she heard the soft click of the library door opening. She looked up and noticed, without much surprise, Lord Royce himself standing there, a pile of papers in his arms.

Despite the slight chill in the air, he was in his shirtsleeves, his hair falling in a rumpled mass to his shoulders. He looked startled to see her there, and, for one second, the candle in his hand wavered.

"Lord Royce," she said with a smile. "We really must stop meeting like this."

"Miss Richards," he answered slowly. "I did not expect anyone to be about at this hour."

"I could not sleep, so I came down here to find something to read."

"And what did you find? A novel?" He came closer to the desk, put his candle down next to hers and the papers atop some books, and sat in the chair beside her. He smelled of clean soap and night air; his warmth and nearness was natural, comforting.

"No. It is the first volume of your series on ancient Greece."

"Indeed?" His dark brow arched. "What do you think of my work, Miss Richards? Too stuffy and academic?"

Cassie shook her head. "You are a very talented

writer, Lord Royce," she said quietly. "I could almost imagine myself there."

"That is a very kind thing for you to say."

"It is not kindness. It is the truth. Through your words, I can see the marketplace in my mind. Smell the wine and olive oil, feel the Grecian sun on my face, and hear all the chatter and laughter." Cassie looked back down at the open book. "In a strange way, it reminded me of—of Jamaica."

"Of Jamaica? Ancient Greece? In what way?"

She wondered if he was making fun of her. After all, ancient Greece and Jamaica were really nothing alike. But when she glanced up at him, she saw only interest written on his face. "In the way so much of life is lived outdoors. In the warmth of the sun, and the diet of fish and fruit and wine. When I was a child, Antoinette's mother would take us to the market in Negril with her. I remember how much I loved that, how I loved the sights and smells, being surrounded by all the *life* . . ."

Her throat grew tight, and she lapsed into silence.

"You miss it very much, don't you?" he said quietly.

"England is not so very bad," Cassie answered. "It has its own sort of life. But yes, I do sometimes get homesick, even now."

"Why did you not stay on there?"

"My parents were gone; Antoinette was all I had left. And Aunt Chat wrote so often, urging me to come stay with her. It seemed the best thing to do." Cassie ran her hand over the cool smoothness of the paper. "There *are* women who can run their own plantations and succeed. But I do not think I could be one of them."

"I think you could do anything you set your mind to," he said.

Cassie looked up at him, startled. No one had ever said anything like that to her before. No one had ever thought her capable, or sensible, or able to do much of anything. Even her parents and Antoinette, who loved her, never had. "You do? Truly?"

"Truly."

"Then I shall have to set my mind to something." She closed the book and looked down at his name embossed on the cover. "I wish I could write a book, like you."

"You could probably write a grand horrid novel," he suggested. "Strange noises in the night, mysterious servants. Exotic ceremonies in seaside tunnels."

Cassie grinned at him. "Oh, so you have heard about that scheme, have you?"

He grinned back. "My mother said something to me about it. She also said I could come along, if I like."

"Of course you can come along. They are your tunnels, after all. But no cynical comments, if you please."

"The spirits won't appear if there is an unfriendly presence, eh?"

"Something of the sort."

"Then I promise, no comments of any sort. You read my book; the least I can do is be polite at your—ceremony."

"I learned a great deal from your book, Lord Royce," Cassie said. "Perhaps you can learn something from me."

He looked at her steadily, his eyes serious. "I am sure I can, Miss Richards."

Cassie returned his regard for a long, still moment. The room around them seemed to disappear. Books, ghosts, castles, Jamaica—nothing else existed in the world for that one instant. Nothing but him and herself, held together in a strange accord.

It should have been an uncomfortable moment, a nervous thing. Yet it was not. It just felt—right. Completely right, to be here with this man, in this moment, alone in the quiet of the night.

Then he looked away, and the odd enchantment was broken. Cassie, too, glanced away, afraid she might be overcome with this strange emotion, these vague yearnings, and start to cry.

"Why must we go specifically to the tunnels on Friday?" he asked in a strained voice. Then he leaned back casually in his chair, his arms crossed, and Cassie thought she must have imagined that hoarse tone, that moment of intimacy. "Why not the drawing room or the breakfast room?"

He could not be feeling the same way she was. He was logical and rational; she was prone to flights of romance and fancy.

She tried to focus her mind on his question. "Antoinette says that the phase of the moon will be just right on Friday, and somehow her fainting episode told her that the tunnels are the right place. I fear I have not studied these things as she has, so I could not tell you why that is. You will just have to come and see for yourself."

"Oh, I shall. I am quite looking forward to it." The old tone of doubt was back in his voice, in his expression.

Cassie could feel them falling back into what was already a familiar pattern, and she was grateful for it. She would need time alone, time when she was not so confused, to examine these strange new feelings. "And so am I, Lord Royce. Very much."

"You know, 'Lord Royce' sounds terribly formal, considering our circumstances. Perhaps you could call me Phillip? Just when we are alone?" He sounded quite endearingly shy and hesitant as he asked this, not at all like his usual self.

Cassie's eyes widened in surprise at this informality. "Call you—Phillip?"

"Well, you do not have to, of course. It just sounds ridiculous for you to be calling me Lord Royce all the time."

"I should like to call you Phillip. When we are—informal like this. Perhaps you could also call me Cassandra."

He smiled at her. "Very well, then, it is a bargain—Cassandra."

She smiled, too. Her name on his lips sounded different than when anyone else had ever said it. It sounded exotic and elegant, and very sweet.

"Would you care to go riding with me tomorrow, Cassandra?" he continued. "Mother has assigned me to deliver some invitations to the masked ball to her friends in the village. You could meet some of them."

"I would like that very much, Phillip. Thank you." Then the little clock on the fireplace mantel struck two. Cassie looked at it in surprise. "Is it so late already? I should retire."

"Yes," he answered. "So should I."

Cassie stood up, still holding the book in her hands. "Would you mind if I borrowed this? I would like to finish reading it."

"Not at all. Keep it as long as you like."

"Well, then. Good night." Then she hurried off to her own chamber, the book clutched very tightly against her.

Phillip watched Cassie leave, then sat down in her vacated chair behind the desk.

The faint scent of her perfume still clung to the

air. Phillip shook his head to try to clear it of the enchantment of that fragrance.

What a very odd night it had been. He had been unable to sleep, unable even to stay still in his bed. Something in his mind had kept urging him to get up, to go to the library. He had thought it was just an urge to work, something that came on him rather often late at night.

Then he walked into the library and saw Miss Richards—Cassandra—sitting there. Her black hair fell loose from where she had tied it back carelessly with a ribbon, and the candlelight gave it the sheen of the ocean at night. Her eyes were wide and dark and startled as she looked up at him.

Phillip usually disliked it when people came into the library, a place he regarded as his own sanctuary. But it seemed strangely *right* to see her there.

It seemed right to see her anywhere in his home. In the short time she had been there, the place had become a brighter and more cheerful place. A place full of interest and variety. He found himself looking forward to going to the tunnels on Friday night, and even to his mother's silly masked ball.

And he did *not* look forward to the day Cassandra would leave Royce Castle, and his old routine of staying in the library almost all day would return.

"You will just have to find a way to keep her here!" a voice echoed in his head. A voice that sounded oddly—feminine.

Was he hearing things now? First he was feeling sentimental about Cassandra Richards, and now this. He was losing his mind. That was all there was to it.

He rubbed his hands over his face wearily. "I am just tired," he muttered. "This is all just a strange dream."

He blew out the candles and went up to bed, deter-

mined to call on the physician if these strange feelings did not go away in the next few days.

Louisa, perched atop the rolling ladder, shook her
head in exasperation. "Men!" she sighed. "Thick as
a plank, every single one of them."

Chapter Thirteen

For once, Cassie was warm in chilly old England as she galloped along a narrow pathway next to Lord Royce.

No, she reminded herself. Not Lord Royce. Phillip.

She laughed aloud as her horse charged ahead, its hooves churning at the soft ground. They jumped over a fallen log, and she ducked under a tree limb that arched overhead.

The limb missed her head, but snatched her hat away. The hat pins pulled through her hair, disarranging the knot, and Cassie reined her horse in.

"Oh, dear me!" she cried, still gasping with laughter. "I am quite sure I would have won the race, if this silly tree had not gotten in my way." She reached up and tried to smooth her hair back into place.

Phillip rose up in his stirrups to snatch the hat off the limb. "It is easy for you to say that now, but I very nearly overtook you. I am sure *I* would have won."

"Ha! You were miles back." Cassie took the hat from his gloved hand. The jaunty little veil was pulled askew, but otherwise it looked in fair shape. "But we shall call it a draw."

"Done. A draw it is. But I thought you said you had not ridden for a long while?"

"I haven't," Cassie answered, placing the hat back on her head and trying to adjust it back to its former rakish angle. "Not since I came to England."

"Then you are a fine horsewoman indeed. I would hate to see you when you are in practice."

"Why, thank you, Lord R—Phillip! What a nice compliment. Your mother would be very proud to see you doing the pretty."

Phillip laughed ruefully. "I would not say it if I did not mean it! I fear I am not very good at 'doing the pretty,' as you call it." He pointed ahead on the path with his riding crop. "The village is just right over that hill."

"Then I am glad our race came to an end," said Cassie. "I would not want people to think I am some hoyden who gallops carelessly along."

"Oh, no, never that." Phillip drew his horse back onto the path at a sedate walk, and Cassie fell in beside him. "There may not be anyone about who could have seen you come galloping in, anyway. The village is rather small, just the church and a few shops, and some of Mother's friends who live at the far end of the road."

"It sounds lovely," said Cassie. "Bath is so very crowded all of the time. It's always exciting, but sometimes . . ." She paused, not sure of the exact word she was looking for.

"Overwhelming?" Phillip suggested.

"Yes, exactly."

"I often feel the same way in cities. Perhaps that is why I usually stay at the castle, though I know Mother would prefer more society."

"She is so looking forward to this masked ball!"

"Indeed she is. And that reminds me of my other errand. I am to take you to the dressmaker so you can order your costume. I think Mother and your aunt have already ordered theirs."

"How grand!" Cassie said with a smile. She already had about fifty ideas for costumes.

They paused at the crest of the hill and looked down at the village. It seemed like a little fairy-tale hamlet from this distance, neat rows of half-timbered buildings and thatched-roofed cottages. Blue-gray smoke curled out of several chimneys, and, despite what Phillip had said, there *were* people about. They strolled along the narrow walkways, and went in and out of shop doors. She could see the square stone tower of the church, and what looked like an inn, and maybe a tea shop.

"It is larger than I expected," she said, smoothing the high collar of her dark green riding habit.

"It has everything we need," Phillip answered.

"Including a bookshop?"

"Especially a bookshop! And, as you can tell, it is not very far from the castle."

Cassie looked back over the way they had come. She could see the castle rising up in the distance, over fields and trees. It seemed a vast expanse of green and gray ground. "Who does all that land belong to?" she asked.

"To me, of course," Phillip answered. "Or rather, to my family."

"Such a lot. My father would have been so envious," she said thoughtfully.

"Did your father not have land in Jamaica?"

"Oh, yes. A great deal, of which I have kept a small parcel, just in case. But he only went out to the West Indies because he was a younger son and had no land here."

"I sometimes wish *I* had an older brother," Phillip said, guiding his horse down the hill.

Cassie followed him. "Do you? Why?"

"Perhaps then I would not have to spend any time with bailiffs and secretaries and lawyers. That would have been my older brother's responsibility."

"And you could spend every bit of your time on writing?"

Phillip smiled at her. "Oh, I don't think I would spend *every* bit of my time writing. Not anymore."

Cassie laughed and had just opened her mouth to answer him, when a voice called, "Lord Royce! What a pleasure to see you in the village on such a fine day."

Cassie turned her head to see a tall, reed-thin man in a neat black coat hurrying toward them.

"Good morning, Mr. Lewisham," Phillip replied, pulling his horse to a halt. He dismounted and reached up to assist Cassie. "Miss Richards, this is our good vicar, Mr. Lewisham, who shepherds the flock at St. Anne's Church most admirably. Mr. Lewisham, this is one of our guests at the castle, Miss Cassandra Richards."

"How do you do, Mr. Lewisham," Cassie said politely.

"A pleasure to meet you, Miss Richards!" Mr. Lewisham replied with a wide smile. "You are the one from Jamaica, are you not?"

"I—well, yes, I am," Cassie said, rather nonplused. She had never seen this man in her life; how did he know where she was from?

Mr. Lewisham laughed. "I did not mean to surprise you, Miss Richards! News travels fast in such a small, isolated place. We have heard all about you and your very unusual companion. And my wife and I have been reading about the West Indies. It is a dream of ours to do missionary work there. You must come and have tea with us, if you have the time before returning to the castle."

"Thank you, Mr. Lewisham," Cassie said. "I should be honored."

"We are to have luncheon with Lady Paige," added Phillip. "But we would be happy to call on Mrs. Lewisham this afternoon."

Mr. Lewisham rubbed his thin hands together in delight. "Excellent! Well, I must be hurrying on now, but I look forward to seeing you later, Lord Royce, Miss Richards." Then he bowed and continued on down the pathway to the road.

"What a nice man," Cassie commented as Phillip led her off toward the livery stable where they could leave their horses. Several other people bowed and smiled as they passed by.

"People in Cornwall have the reputation for being wary of strangers," Phillip answered. "But here you can see that is scarcely the case. I am sure you will be very warmly welcomed everywhere. Or at least *almost* anywhere."

And so she was. Cassie went to visit Mrs. Brown, the dressmaker, while Phillip waited for her at the bookshop. There, in Mrs. Brown's cozy front room, she met four other young ladies. They became so caught up in poring over fashion plates and examining fabrics that she quite lost track of time. Until the bells at the church tolled the hour and she remembered that they were to have luncheon with Lady Royce's friend Lady Paige.

She hastily decided on a blue-and-yellow fabric for her shepherdess's costume, gathered up her other purchases, and hurried out of the shop.

Lord Royce was pacing about on the walkway, a square, book-shaped parcel tucked under his arm.

"Why did you not come inside to fetch me?" Cassie asked, falling into step beside him as they set off down the street. "I met some other ladies, and we started talking, and, well, we rather lost track of time."

Phillip looked back at the pleasant little shop, a look almost of horror on his handsome face. "Me? Go into a—a lady's dressmaker shop?"

Cassie laughed. "Oh, Lord Royce! It is hardly the portal of doom. It is really quite a nice place. I found these delightful blue ribbons . . ."

"Please, my dear Miss Richards," he said in a pained voice. "No talk of ribbons. I beg you."

Cassie laughed again, and tucked her hand in the crook of his arm as they strolled along, meeting other people and glancing into shop windows.

She thought it felt rather odd, as if they were some old married couple.

"My dear Lord Royce! How kind of you to come see me. It has been much too long since I've seen you." Lady Paige, a round little matron in elegant gray silk and a lace cap, went up on tiptoe to peck a kiss on Phillip's cheek.

Phillip bent down, accepting the salute with good grace, and Cassie discerned a hint of a blush on his cheeks. She almost laughed as she hung back in the doorway of Lady Paige's drawing room, waiting to be introduced.

"Far too long, Lady Paige," he answered.

"Pish! You used to call me Aunt Lydia. Now, who is this lovely young lady? The houseguest your mother has told me so much about?" Lady Paige turned her curious gaze onto Cassie.

"Yes, indeed. This is Miss Richards. Miss Richards, may I present my mother's dear friend, Lady Paige?"

"How do you do?" Cassie said politely.

"Oh, Miss Richards, what a delight to meet you! You

are every bit as pretty as Melinda said. You have both chosen a perfect day to come for luncheon, as well."

"Have we, La—Aunt Lydia?" Phillip inquired. "How so?"

"Because my nephew, Mr. Neville Vickery, is here from Town!" Lady Paige clapped her hands together. "He so seldom visits his poor auntie, you know, and he has such vastly amusing stories to tell." She leaned toward Cassie and whispered confidingly, "He is quite the beau, you know. The joy of every young lady's eye! I am sure you will like him, Miss Richards."

Phillip gave her an alarmed look, and Cassie again had the urge to laugh. "I am sure I shall, Lady Paige," she said.

Then they went into Lady Paige's drawing room, a small space crowded with figurines, paintings, and embroidered cushions—and one extraordinary "tulip of fashion."

Cassie giggled behind her hand to think that the young man standing by the window could be the joy of any young lady's eye. He was tall, true, and had pleasing, regular features. But his golden hair was pomaded to such a high gloss that it glowed, his cravat was so elaborately tied that it resembled nothing so much as a wedding cake, and his yellow coat was nearly blinding.

Cassie could not help but glance at Phillip, and compare his plain, serviceable garments and carelessly long hair to the yellow coat and embroidered orange waistcoat. It was all too obvious which man came out with the advantage.

But Lady Paige beamed at her nephew as if he were a veritable Apollo come to earth. "Lord Royce, Miss Richards, may I present my nephew, Mr. Vickery?"

Mr. Vickery moved across the crowded room with a stylish languor, and took Cassie's hand in his. As he raised it to his lips, his many rings cut into Cassie's skin.

"Charmed, I'm sure," he said in a low, drawling voice. "Aunt Lydia, you never told me that there were hidden charms in this pokey old village. I would have come to visit an age ago."

Lady Paige tittered as if he had uttered a great witticism. "Oh, Neville! How you do tease."

Mr. Vickery gave Cassie what he obviously considered a soulful, Byronic look. "I am completely serious. You never said an angel resided in this remote corner."

Laughter threatened to bubble up to Cassie's lips again, and she feared that if she let even another giggle escape she would not be able to stop. Did ladies in London really *enjoy* this sort of ridiculous flattery?

It was amusing, to be sure, but she found that she much preferred Phillip's sensible conversation.

"How very kind you are, Mr. Vickery," she said, carefully extracting her hand from his grasp.

"It is not kindness at all, Miss Richards—merely the truth. Please, let me escort you into the dining room. I am so eager to hear what you think of this bleak corner of the world." Without even waiting for her leave, he took her arm and tugged her out of the room, brushing past Lord Royce and his aunt. "I do hope your cook has not burned the soup today, Aunt Lydia," was his only careless comment to her, tossed back over his shoulder.

"Oh, yes! I mean, no," Lady Paige cried, obviously distressed. "I am sure she has not, after your unhappiness with the fish yesterday, Neville."

"Quite," Mr. Vickery said curtly. He leaned closer

to Cassie and murmured, "It is so very difficult here to maintain proper standards, Miss Richards. Not at all like my house in London. You must allow me to tell you all about it . . ."

Cassie only listened with half an ear as Mr. Vickery, the joy of every young lady's eye, went on about his house in London and all his highborn friends. She watched as Lord Royce seated the slighted Lady Paige in her chair at the head of the table and conversed with her about various village doings. Slowly, the hurt look in her eyes over her nephew's carelessness faded, and a new sparkle took its place. Lord Royce nodded understandingly at her words and smiled.

All traces of the impatient, unsocial scholar vanished. He was all patience and kindness—just as he always was with his mother and Aunt Chat and even Antoinette, who most people treated as a mere curiosity.

As hard as he tried to hide it, Lord Royce was a very kind and thoughtful man. Not even his shabby coats could hide that, just as Mr. Vickery's yellow satin could not hide his shallowness.

Cassie smiled at the revelation, but unfortunately that small lifting of her lips encouraged Mr. Vickery to even greater heights of bragging about his barouche.

Phillip half listened to Lady Paige as he watched Mr. Vickery charming Miss Richards.

A sour, unaccustomed pang ached somewhere in his stomach as he looked at the fashionable man leaning close to her, speaking into her ear. She gave a small, almost intimate smile at whatever it was he was saying.

Mr. Vickery must be a riveting conversationalist,

Phillip thought, as well as a sparkling dresser. His yellow coat, though a bilious color, was perfectly cut, his linen impeccably free of ink stains. No doubt he could converse on many subjects other than the ancient Greeks. How could a lady help but be impressed with him?

Phillip ruefully inspected the frayed cuff of his coat. Perhaps, just perhaps, he should visit the tailor and have some new ones made up. Not in yellow, to be sure, but maybe a sensible blue or brown. What would Miss Richards think of him then?

Phillip brusquely dismissed that thought just as it flitted through his mind. He did not have time for such frivolities! His coats had been good enough for months.

But still, a small voice whispered at the back of his mind, if a new coat could make her smile at him as she was smiling now, it could be worth it.

It could be worth it, indeed.

"How did you find my old friend Lady Paige and her nephew?" Lady Royce asked over supper that night at Royce Castle. "Is she enjoying living in the village? Did she accept the invitation to the masked ball?"

"She was very well, Mother, and of course she accepted the invitation," answered Phillip. "Everyone we invited accepted, did they not, Miss Richards?"

"Oh, yes," Cassie said, happy for the excuse to abandon her fillet of sole. The fish was excellent, but after an unusually large luncheon at Lady Paige's house, and tea and cakes with the Lewishams, she was quite stuffed. "All the people we met were so very kind! I had a wonderful day." And she had. Even Mr. Vickery, in his own way, had been very amusing. Cassie laughed, recalling his attempts at flirtation over luncheon.

Lady Royce beamed. "Yes, it is a very nice neighborhood. We should have everyone to the castle more often, should we not, Phillip?"

He looked at his mother suspiciously, as if he thought she might be up to something. "Of course, Mother."

Lady Royce nodded. "And did you get to go to Mrs. Brown's shop, my dear Miss Richards? She does such lovely work. I really think she could go to London."

"She did have some very pretty samples," Cassie agreed. "I ordered a couple of gowns as well as my costume."

"Did you decide on something, then, Cassie?" Antoinette asked.

"I am going to be a shepherdess," Cassie answered. "Have *you* decided on something?"

Antoinette shook her head. "I told you. It is a surprise."

"I am going to be Queen Elizabeth," Lady Royce offered. "And Chat will be Eleanor of Aquitaine. But Phillip still will not tell me what his costume is to be."

Phillip smiled. "That is because I do not know yet. I would rather not wear a costume at all."

"Of course you must wear a costume! That is the fun of it." Lady Royce sighed happily. "Oh, I *am* looking forward to this so very much!"

Chapter Fourteen

"Tell me, Louisa, why do you want to find Lady Lettice so much? I mean, why her in particular?" Cassie asked. They were walking along the shore toward the tunnels, on their way to Antoinette's ceremony. Antoinette, Chat, and Lady Royce hurried ahead, carrying Antoinette's books, herbs, and candles, while Lord Royce trailed far behind.

He did not even appear to see Louisa at all, but Cassie thought it seemed quite normal to be in her company now. It could have been any evening stroll, really, if only her companion did not float above the sand rather than walk on it.

Louisa paused for a moment, then answered, "We want to know where they go."

"Where they go?"

"The ghosts who only stay for a brief while, and the people who die and do not become ghosts at all, like my husband. Sir Belvedere and I are the only ones who have stayed here so long, and we often wonder why. We just thought Lady Lettice might be the most likely to return, since she was here a rather long time as well."

Cassie nodded. She, too, would like to know where they had all gone. Perhaps then she would know about her parents.

Louisa paused and turned her head to look out at the moonlit sea. The hood of her cloak hid her face. "I just want to *know*," she whispered.

Cassie reached out to squeeze her hand, but felt only cool air. "If anyone can find out, it is Antoinette."

"Yes. Of course," said Louisa, her voice cheerful in a rather determined way. Then she looked ahead and gave a little, glowing wave. "Look! There is Sir Belvedere, waiting at the tunnel." She floated away, leaving Cassie standing alone on the shore.

She shivered a bit and pulled her red cloak closer about her. She *did* want to know, just as much as Louisa did. If she could just know that her parents were at peace, that they were together again . . .

But there was also a part of her that didn't really want to know at all. A very tiny part that was afraid.

Phillip came up beside her and gently touched her arm. "Having second thoughts?" he said softly.

Cassie looked up at him. The moonlight gave a silvery cast to his handsome face, making him look even more beautiful and rather otherworldly. Everything seemed cast in unreality tonight, even this solid, logical man.

She drew herself up to her full height, only to find that she still barely came to his shoulder. "Of course not," she said stoutly. "Are you? Oh, no, *you* would not be. You think nothing is going to happen tonight."

"I never said that. I simply do not *know* what is going to happen."

He looked to the tunnels, where the others had already gone in. The light of their lanterns and candles sent a golden wash out of the entrance onto the rocks and sand.

Cassie studied him carefully. Did he feel it, too, then? This sense that tonight was—special.

He smiled down at her and held out his arm. "Shall we, then?"

She nodded and slipped her hand onto the sleeve of his greatcoat, grateful for its warm solidity beneath her touch. And she knew then that, no matter what happened, she would be safe with him at her side.

"Oh, spirits of the night, of the sea and air! Hear my summons. Come to me!"

Antoinette's voice, deep and resonant, echoed in the dim, shallow tunnel. They had put out their lanterns, and the smoke from the circle of candles stung Cassie's eyes. She rubbed them before opening them again to look around her.

Antoinette stood in the middle of the circle of lights, her eyes half-closed, her mother's book open at her feet. She swayed slightly as she murmured, her green robe shimmering in the light. The others were gathered in a ragged oval outside the lights, holding hands and watching Antoinette with wide eyes.

There was a palpable air of tension and expectation in the still, cold air. No one knew what was going to happen next, and everyone looked about with nervous, darting little glances before looking at Antoinette again.

Cassie saw Aunt Chat look toward the tunnel entrance, her expression full of longing. Her hand tugged slightly in Cassie's grasp, but Cassie gave it a reassuring squeeze and she turned back to the group.

Phillip's hand lay still and warm in Cassie's other hand, his palm slightly rough against her skin. He, too, watched Antoinette closely, with a small, puzzled frown on his face. He looked as if he was listening to a rather fascinating lecture at Oxford.

Cassie wished she could be as calm as he was, as clinical. Her stomach felt fluttery and tight, and her hands were cold. As Antoinette's voice became louder, her words faster, Cassie longed to throw herself into Phillip's arms and shout out for her to stop.

She had even moved a step closer to him, tugging Aunt Chat with her, when a loud explosion echoed from the back of the tunnel. Bright blue-green light flashed, followed by a shower of sparks.

Cassie screamed and really did fall into Phillip's arms. He held her tightly against him, and she buried her face in the starchy, clean scent of his shirtfront.

But she couldn't help peeking back at the tunnel.

Antoinette ceased her chanting, and stared, mouth agape, at the darkness beyond the candles. Chat and Lady Royce clung to each other, also staring. Chat, unflappable Aunt Chat, trembled under her Indian print shawl. Louisa and Sir Belvedere, hovering near the entrance, watched with avid eyes.

In the wake of the brilliant explosion, the back of the tunnel seemed even darker than before. A faint drift of smoke floated to the ceiling.

Then a woman stepped forward, with a little, childlike man holding on to her hand. She was quite an amazing vision, tall and slim, with dark red hair coiled atop her head and crowned with a red velvet, pearl-trimmed cap. She wore a red satin gown in the Elizabethan style, richly embroidered, spread wide over a drum farthingale, with a tall, lacy ruff framing her pale, glowing face.

She stared back at them, faintly bewildered. It was deeply quiet in the tunnel.

Phillip pulled Cassie closer to him, and her hands

tightened on the wool of his greatcoat. She couldn't breathe from wondering what might happen next.

The little man-child the woman held by the hand leaped up and down, the bells on his blue velvet cap and doublet jingling discordantly. He tugged at the woman's beringed hand and cried, "What is happening, Lady Lettice? Angelo is confused!"

"Hush, Angelo," the woman said quietly, taking in their gaping gathering with one sweeping glance. Then she saw Louisa and Sir Belvedere, and her eyes widened.

"Louisa," she said, her voice low and calm. "Sir Belvedere. So lovely to see you again. Have you moved on, or have I returned to Royce Castle?" Before they could answer, she glided forward, her skirts rustling silkily, the little man tugged in her wake. "But I can see that I am back at the castle. I remember these tunnels. Oh, indeed I do."

"Hello, Lettice," said Louisa.

"Fair Lady Lettice," Sir Belvedere said, then did one of his clanking bows. "We are very happy to see you again."

"Are you?" Lettice murmured. She looked at Antoinette, who still stood in her circle of lights. "And I suppose *you* are the one who brought me here?"

Antoinette tilted her chin back, her eyes narrowed as she examined Lettice. "I am Miss Antoinette Duvall," she answered. "I *am* the one who summoned you."

Lettice frowned, her pale forehead puckering under the widow's peak of her hair. "But whatever for?"

"It was at our request," Louisa said. "We wanted to see you again."

"Did you?" Lettice asked, still looking most puzzled. Then Angelo pulled at her hand again and squealed, "Angelo is hungry, my lady! They took me away from my cakes and ale."

"Hush, Angelo. You are always hungry." Lettice pressed one hand on her throat, clattering the long strands of pearls and rubies there. "I need to leave these tunnels!"

She floated quickly out into the night, along with the noisy Angelo. Louisa and Sir Belvedere followed her, leaving the humans alone.

Cassie pulled away from Phillip to look up at his face. She expected to see him scornful and doubting, perhaps with his brow raised or a cynical little smile on his lips.

Instead, he was almost as pale as Lady Lettice. He stared unseeing into the depths of the tunnel, where the ghosts had appeared.

Cassie reached up and gently touched his cheek, bringing his gaze back to her. His skin was cold. "Phillip?" she whispered.

He placed his hand over hers, holding it to his cheek. "This is some sort of dream, is it not, Cassandra? A dream that has you in it, as well. I knew I should not have eaten that mushroom tart at supper."

"It is not a dream," Cassie answered. "I told you Antoinette has powers, but you did not believe me. Now you can see that there really *are* spirits, right here in your very home."

He frowned. "How do I know that these people are not actors you have hired to play out this little scene?"

His mother heard his words. She pulled away from Chat and straightened her cloak over her shoulders. She, too, was a bit pale, but her eyes were bright with excitement. "Don't be so ridiculous, Phillip! How could we get them to fly? To glow? And why would we go to so much trouble just to play a joke on *you*? My dear, you are just going to have to face the fact that there are things in this world that your books cannot explain. That logic cannot dismiss."

With a decisive little nod, she hurried out of the tunnel in search of the ghosts. Chat followed her.

Antoinette was gathering up her book and herbs, her dark face suffused with joy. "I did it!" she murmured as she blew out most of the candles. "I truly did it. Oh, I wish Mama could see this!"

And, she, too, left the tunnel, not even seeing Phillip and Cassie still standing there.

In the cold gloom, Phillip staggered over to an old upturned crate and sat down on it heavily. "So it was not a dream?" he muttered. "How can that be? What was it?"

Cassie was very worried. He did not sound at all like his usual scholarly self. He sounded, and looked, like a little lost boy.

She thought with a fright that perhaps the shock had undone him. She hurried over to his side and pulled the collar of his coat closer about his throat.

"It is all right," she soothed. "Quite all right. Spirits have always been with us, even in ancient Greece. *They* believed in spirits, too, did they not?" She wasn't exactly sure if they had or not, but she certainly hoped it was so. If only she had finished reading his book!

"Rational thinkers rejected such superstitions," he said uncertainly.

"Would you doubt the rationality of your own eyes?" Cassie argued. "Did you not see them yourself? Right here? And they cannot be a dream or hallucination, because we all saw them."

Phillip took her hand and looked up steadily into

her eyes. "But what *are* they? Tell me, Cassandra. I must know."

Cassie shook her head. This was something she had wondered herself, but then she had come to the conclusion that it was simply unknowable. "I do not know exactly. They are the spirits of people who have lived here before, but I don't know why they are still here. *They* do not even know. But perhaps Lady Lettice can tell us something."

He shook his head and pulled away from her. The color had returned to his face, but now he looked angry and confused. He stood up and paced across the tunnel, his arms crossed. "Then if you cannot tell me the purpose, the truth, of this, why have you done it?"

"Because we do *not* know, of course!" Cassie said, confused. She had seen him cynical and doubting, and stuffy and smart, but never angry. Now he strolled the narrow periphery of the tunnel, kicking out at the extinguished candles, the spent piles of herbs. "We— we thought we might learn something . . ."

"Did you have to do it here?" he said, staring at her with burning eyes. "Perhaps things of this sort are usual in Jamaica, but we are in England. This has no place in a civilized, ordered society." He gave her one more glare for good measure. "No place."

Then he turned and stormed out of the tunnel.

Cassie was stunned. She would not have guessed that Phillip had such depths of temper in him. She had disrupted the calm, unruffled order of his life, and now he was unsure. She completely understood his feelings.

But *why* did he have to take out his anger on her? She had meant no harm at all. She had only wanted to help him see beyond his blasted logic, to expand his horizons.

It appeared she had made a great mistake. After all, some people did not want their horizons expanded. She would not have thought that Phillip, a scholar, would be one of them.

Her eyes stung with unshed tears. She wiped at them fiercely with the back of her hand, squared her shoulders, and marched out of the tunnel. Standing about feeling sorry for herself would do no one any good at all.

And she was not about to let such an old fusty-musty as Lord Royce ruin her pleasure in the successful ceremony!

On the beach, the four ghosts were gathered near the water, whispering and gesturing. The only thing that could be heard from them was the clatter of Sir Belvedere's armor and the jingle of Angelo's bells.

Antoinette was sitting down on a large rock, looking thoroughly exhausted but also exultant. She held her mother's book against her, stroking her hand over the worn leather cover.

Chat and Lady Royce hovered near her, talking excitedly. When Cassie emerged into the moonlight, they hurried over to her.

"Cassie, dear, are you quite all right?" Chat said worriedly. "We saw Lord Royce come stomping past earlier. Did you quarrel?"

Cassie gave them a weak smile. "He is rather angry over what happened tonight. I tried to talk to him, but . . ."

"Of course he is angry!" Lady Royce cried. "He would never listen to me before, never even consider that the castle might be haunted. Now he has been proven wrong, proven wrong by *women*, and he is upset. Such a man. I cannot believe I raised him."

Cassie thought there was probably more to it than

that, but she was too tired to talk about it, or even think about it any more tonight.

"I am sure you are right, Lady Royce," she answered.

"We will all talk to him tomorrow," Lady Royce said. "I am sure he will see sense in the clear light of day." She did not seem to realize the irony of having ghosts be "sense."

"You should be in your bed, dear," said Chat. "You and Antoinette both look thoroughly exhausted."

Cassie let herself be led away along the shore; her feet felt like lead in her boots. It *had* been a long, eventful, tiring evening.

Before they turned away to climb the steps up the cliff, she looked back over her shoulder at the gathering of ghosts. Louisa caught her eye and gave her a cheerful little wave.

Cassie waved back. At least *someone* seemed happy about the proceedings.

Chapter Fifteen

"So you know nothing of what happens when we leave here?" Louisa asked Lady Lettice. "Nothing at all?"

Lady Lettice shook her head. "Only what I have told you. Angelo and I were in a sort of sitting room the entire time. It was rather pleasant. There were always people to play cards with, especially that nice Roman gentleman, Didius."

"There was ale and cakes!" Angelo cried. "And roast beef and peacock . . ."

Lady Lettice tugged impatiently at his hand, and he lapsed into quiet mutters. "And sugared almonds and stewed quail and puddings . . ." he whispered, kicking at the pebbles with the upturned toe of his shoe.

"There *was* plenty of food," Lady Lettice said. "Sometimes a man would come and ask us very impertinent questions, and write things down. But I do not know why I was there, or why I returned, except that you summoned me."

"And you did not see—well, anyone *interesting* there?" Louisa asked haltingly.

Lady Lettice gave her a knowing look. "Someone like your William, perhaps?"

"He was not *my* William," Louisa cried indignantly. "Not even when he was alive."

Lady Lettice nodded. "Be that as it may, I did not see him. Or indeed anyone I knew except Angelo. It was sometimes rather dull, despite the food and cards and Didius, so I cannot say I am completely sorry to be back at Royce Castle. Especially with such interesting people in residence. Who is the dark-skinned female who summoned me here? Does she live in the castle?"

Louisa looked over to where the humans had disappeared over the crest of the cliffs. Their figures could be seen faintly, moving up the path to the castle. "That is Miss Antoinette Duvall, from Jamaica. She is visiting here with Miss Cassandra Richards and Lady Willowby, Miss Richards' aunt. Miss Richards is also from Jamaica; we have had interesting discussions about it. I wish that ghosts could choose where they travel, so I could see it for myself. They *believe* in ghosts there!"

"Does anyone really live in such a wild place as that?" Lady Lettice asked coolly, lifting up a small feathered fan from where it dangled on her belt and waving it languidly. "I heard in my lifetime that there was nothing but savages there. I would rather still be in the sitting room of the afterlife than go to Jamaica."

As Louisa looked at her, she remembered what a snobbish wench Lady Lettice could be at times. She wondered why she had ever wanted her summoned back.

"Angelo would like to see Jamaica," Lady Lettice's dwarf piped up. "There is fruit there as big as your head! And fish to be cooked in spices and rum . . ."

Lady Lettice smiled down at him fondly and patted the top of his head. "Angelo, my chuck, you think far too much about food. Ghosts cannot even eat here on earth!"

"Angelo can *remember* eating," he mumbled. "We *could* eat in the sitting room of the afterlife."

"Well, we are here now, and it is impossible to eat in our present form. Now, Louisa, Sir Belvedere," Lady Lettice said decisively, dropping her fan and turning to face them. "It appears I have arrived just in time. Things at Royce Castle seem to be getting completely unruly. Let us go up to my chamber, which I hope has been aired and cleaned properly, and you may tell me all about what has been going on here." Then her voice changed from its usual strident tones to a soft purr. "Especially about that handsome gentleman with the long, dark hair . . ."

Phillip locked the door to the library behind him and hurried over to the table, where the butler left various decanters and glasses every evening. Usually he did not touch them at all, but tonight was a marked exception. He poured himself a generous measure of brandy and gulped it down as if it was water. Then he poured out another one.

What was happening to him? Here, in his very home, the place he regarded as a haven from the insanity of the outside world! Now it seemed that that very hysteria, the wildness of the so-called Romantics, had reached between the stones of Royce Castle and grabbed onto him.

Clutching at his brandy, he sat down in the chair behind the desk and looked about at the library. It all seemed the same; the same neat rows of books, the same dark furniture, the same painting over the fireplace. His notes and volumes were all in tidy little piles on the desk. But he felt dazed, disturbed. Completely out of sorts.

These were feelings he disliked intensely. He liked to know his purpose, his place in the world. He liked his household to be in order, to know what he could expect from every day.

That was gone now, vanished in that blast of blue-green light. If he was to be honest with himself, he would have to admit that it had been gone before that, since the day Cassandra Richards stepped past his threshold. She was making him doubt things he had always believed—things such as logic, order, rationality. She had made unfamiliar feelings rise up inside him—desires for picnics, wild rides, and myths and stories.

And now he had actually engaged in some sort of mass hysteria in the tunnel. The fact that they *all* believed they saw a ghost had infected his own mind and made him believe it, as well.

That had to be all there was to it.

He could not have actually seen some supernatural being. He shook his head stubbornly. That could not be.

He took another sip of the brandy and reflected that soon he would have his peaceful, scholarly life back again. After the blasted masked ball, Cassie and her aunt and her strange friend would surely return to Bath, leaving him to get on with his work.

Through the warm brandy haze, he wondered why that thought did not comfort him as it should. In fact, it did not comfort him at all.

"Handsome but stupid, I see," Lady Lettice commented, watching him from atop the rolling ladder next to Louisa. "Some of the best men are, of course. Sir Francis Drake, for one, was really very thick. But one does hope for more from someone who is meant to be a scholar. Now, if you had known Sir Phillip Sidney . . ."

"Yes, yes," Louisa interrupted impatiently. She had forgotten how Lady Lettice tended to go on and on about all the famous people she had once known. "But what do you think of my idea, Lady Lettice?"

"Of matching up this man with your Miss Richards from Jamaica?" Lady Lettice tapped at her chin thoughtfully with her feather fan. One thing she had always been rather fond of was making matches; Louisa knew that very well. She thought perhaps it was to compensate for having never been married herself. And now Louisa hoped to engage her in this mission.

"The free spirit and the stuffy scholar," Lady Lettice went on. "I think it has great potential, my dear Louisa. Very amusing potential, indeed. Now, all we have to do is come up with a plan."

Louisa grinned. "Oh, yes. Sir Belvedere and I have been thinking on that . . ."

Chapter Sixteen

"Oh, how marvelous!" Lady Royce cried. She had been reading the morning post over breakfast, and now held up a sheet of parchment with a pleased exclamation.

"What is it, Melinda?" asked Chat, picking a piece of toast out of the rack.

"My dear friend Lady Paige, the one Miss Richards met on her excursion into the village, is having a small supper tonight to bid farewell to her nephew, who is returning to Town. We are all invited." Lady Royce refolded the invitation carefully and smiled. "This *is* splendid, is it not? I have not been out to dine in ever so long."

"Will there be many people there?" Chat asked. "Is it very formal?"

"Oh, no, not at all. Lady Paige's dining room is not big enough for a large party. I am certain Viscount and Viscountess Rockley will be there, and Mrs. Sattler and her daughter, and perhaps the Lewishams."

"It sounds delightful. Does it not, girls?" Chat said,

and glanced down the table to where Cassie and Antoinette sat quietly.

Antoinette, whose dark eyes were heavy with weariness after the exertions of the night before, nodded and murmured her assent.

Cassie looked over at Phillip, who just continued eating his sausages and said nothing. He just barely nodded in his mother's direction. He, too, seemed weary, with dark circles beneath his eyes. Cassie had wondered all night and morning what his reaction might be to the night's occurrences.

Now she knew. He was not taking it at all well.

He had greeted them politely when he entered the breakfast room, but had said barely a word since. He had scarcely even glanced at Cassie.

Perhaps he was just tired, as they all were, she tried to reassure herself. But she still wished he would at least smile at her and talk with her as they had that night in the library. They could discuss what had happened in the tunnels, try to figure out what it all meant.

But it was all too clear that he did not want to talk with her about anything right now, least of all what had happened. He appeared intent on denying it.

Cassie turned her attention back to her plate, listening as Lady Royce planned what she would wear to the supper party. Later, when Phillip was not so tired, she would seek him out and talk to him.

They had so many things to discuss.

"Hm. I do see what Louisa means," Lady Lettice muttered as she watched the scene in the breakfast room. Rather than perch on one of the cornices, as Louisa and Sir Belvedere liked to do, she peered out from one of the portraits. It was much more dignified in a farthingale. "He is a terribly stubborn man. He does not believe in us, even though he saw us with his own eyes, and he blames the poor girl for making him see the truth he will not acknowledge. She certainly has a streak of stubbornness, as well." She peered at them closer. "Yes, indeed, this will be a challenge. Much more so than when I matched up Lettice Knollys and Robert Dudley."

Angelo tugged at her skirts. "Angelo wants some of those sausages! They smell so wonderful."

"Hush, Angelo! I told you yesterday, ghosts cannot eat. You do not really feel hungry, you just think you do," she said distractedly.

"No! Angelo is *really* hungry."

Lady Lettice did not answer; she was too busy listening to the humans' conversation. "They are going to a supper tonight. An excellent opportunity. There are far too many of them for just one carriage; we shall have to see that Lord Royce and Miss Richards are alone in one."

"Angelo does not think a well-bred girl would be alone in a carriage with a man," he said thoughtfully. "Look at what happened to Katherine Throckmorton."

"Then we shall just have to see to it that they are *made* to be alone," Lady Lettice answered impatiently. She took hold of Angelo's hand and floated off. "Now we must find Louisa and Sir Belvedere. They are probably lazing the morning away, playing chess in that East Tower, when there is work to be done!"

"And maybe we will run into Jean-Pierre on the way," Angelo said slyly. His dark eyes flashed with a usually hidden intelligence.

Lady Lettice reached out with her free hand and cuffed him soundly on the head. "Never mention that name to me again! Jean-Pierre is—was a toad.

And he is not a ghost, anyway. He has moved on. We shall never see him here."

But her mind whispered doubtfully, *Will you indeed*?

"What will you wear to Lady Paige's supper, Cassie?" Antoinette said, riffling through the contents of Cassie's wardrobe.

"I don't know," Cassie murmured indifferently, turning over a page of the poetry book she was ostensibly reading. In truth, she had not even read a single word in fully half an hour. "What are you going to wear?"

"Probably that yellow gown your aunt bought for me in Bath. I would not want to go frightening all the guests in my robes!" Antoinette laughed. "They will be frightened enough of me as it is!"

Cassie also laughed and put aside her book. "Well, I do not care what I wear. You choose something for me."

"What about this one?" Antoinette pulled out a sapphire-blue silk. "You loved it when you ordered it from the modiste, and you haven't worn it yet."

"Perhaps."

"Perhaps? Don't you want to look pretty for Lord Royce?" Antoinette held the gown up to herself, even though it was a foot too short, and danced about the room. "Oh, Lord Royce, you are *so* handsome," she cooed in a strange, high-pitched Jamaican accent. "Won't you please, please dance with me?"

Cassie tossed a cushion at her, laughing helplessly. "Antoinette, stop! There won't *be* any dancing tonight. It is just supper and maybe some cards."

"But you will still want to look nice, no? So you should wear this." Antoinette laid the gown out on the bed and smoothed the shimmering folds.

Cassie sighed. "I do not think Lord Royce would notice me if I showed up in my chemise."

"Oh, I do think he would notice *that*." Antoinette came and sat down at the end of the chaise where Cassie lay. Cassie slid her feet back to make room for her. "What is the matter, Cassie? Did you and Lord Royce quarrel?"

"Of course not. You cannot quarrel with a person when they won't speak to you. He was so very quiet at breakfast and would not even look at me. Then, when I went to the library to talk to him, the door was locked. The butler said he had orders that no one was to go in today." Cassie felt her chin wobble and clenched her teeth together. "Probably especially me."

"Oh, Cassie dear," Antoinette replied. "Lord Royce has had a shock. He has spent so many years denying the existence of the supernatural, and last night he came face-to-face with it. Of course he does not feel well. He is probably still denying the whole thing. We have seen this many times, remember?"

Cassie nodded. She remembered some of the people they had known in Jamaica, people who had been there for a long time and had seen much. They lived in fear of voodoo rituals and slave revolts.

"At least that fear is not as dangerous here as it was there," Antoinette finished.

"Yes. But what should I do about Lord Royce? If I could just talk to him . . ."

"Give him time. He will come around, probably sooner than you would think. After all, he is falling in love with you. He will listen to you."

Cassie stared at her friend, shocked. "In—in love with me? Of course he is not! He can barely be civil with me."

"A sure sign that he is in love, then." Antoinette

smiled and stood up to cross the room to the door of her own chamber. "We should be getting changed. We have to leave for Lady Paige's house in an hour."

Almost an hour later, they all stood about in the drive, waiting for the carriages to be brought around. Cassie shivered in her cloak as a chill wind swept across her, and she looked over to where Lord Royce—she could no longer think of him as Phillip— stood, slightly apart from the others.

He did not look angry or upset at all. Merely distantly polite and distracted, as if he was thinking of something else and did not see them.

And looking so handsome in his evening clothes, with his hair sleekly tied back.

Cassie sighed and looked away from him, trying to attend to the conversation of Lady Royce, Aunt Chat, and Antoinette. But all she could hear were Antoinette's previous words echoing in her mind— "He is falling in love with you, you know."

Well, if he *was* he had a very funny way of showing it! Being argumentative and cool by turns was not Cassie's idea of falling in love.

She firmly turned her back to him, determined to enjoy her evening despite him.

"Ah, here come the carriages now!" Lady Royce said, gathering her fur-trimmed wrap around her. "I have ordered two carriages for tonight, so we needn't all be squashed together and crush our gowns. Chat and I will take the first one, and, Phillip, you may escort Miss Richards and Miss Duvall in the other."

Cassie thought she heard a soft giggle in her ear, but when she turned to look, Antoinette stood some distance away, and Aunt Chat and Lady Royce were already climbing into their carriage.

"Louisa?" she whispered, wondering if the ghosts were playing some sort of joke that involved being invisible.

"Did you say something, miss?" asked the footman, who had just stepped forward to help her into the carriage.

Cassie looked around one more time, but saw only Lord Royce, who watched her quizzically. "No," she said, taking the footman's arm and stepping up into the dim interior of the equipage. "Not at all."

She had just settled herself on the soft leather cushion, when there was a strange sort of yell, and Lord Royce tumbled headfirst into the carriage. He landed with a hard thud on the floor at her feet.

"Lord Royce!" she cried. "Whatever is the . . ."

Her exclamations were interrupted when the door slammed shut behind him and the carriage jolted into motion. It gathered speed quickly as it set off down the drive.

Cassie heard muffled shouts from outside. After making sure Phillip was not hurt, she lowered the window and stuck her head out to see the footman, Antoinette, and—oh, horrors!—the coachman chasing after them. Antoinette's expression was frantic as she pointed at the carriage.

Cassie twisted about and saw there was no one sitting on the box at all. The horses were running off on their own.

Her heart lifted into her throat with a cold, frightened leap. She fell back against the seat, gasping. They were going to go right over the cliffs in this runaway carriage and become ghosts who were trapped at Royce Castle forever!

Phillip hauled himself up off the floor and onto the seat opposite her, his hair falling loose onto his shoulders and his cravat askew. "Someone pushed me in here!" he muttered indignantly, as if not even aware that they were moving at a dangerous speed.

"We have worse troubles than that!" Cassie practically screamed, lunging across the space between them to grab onto his coat. "No one is driving this carriage!"

"What?" he said, frowning in confusion. "That cannot be."

"Of course it is! I saw it with my own eyes. No one is on the box."

He pressed her gently back onto her seat and stuck his head out the window. Then he fell back beside her, his expression unreadable. "You are right," he shouted over the rush of cold wind that swirled around them from the open window. "No one is driving this carriage."

"What are we going to do?" Cassie asked frantically.

"I have to try to get up onto the box myself and slow the horses." Phillip looked back out the window. "But I do wonder one thing."

Cassie wondered one thing, too—she wondered how he could be so calm in the face of impending doom. "What?"

"Why is our carriage running away so perfectly down the road? Why are we not crashing through the woods?"

Cassie peered past his shoulder to the flashing-by scenery. He was right. They were going in a straight line down the road, away from the village and the castle.

She frowned. *Louisa*! Of course it had to be Louisa and Sir Belvedere and probably that new Lady Lettice and her dwarf friend.

No one had ever told her that dead people could be so mischievous.

She leaned out the window again, and this time she saw Sir Belvedere sitting up on the box, his armored legs held stiffly before him, wielding the reins. Louisa sat beside him, her blue cloak billowing in the wind.

"What are you doing?" Cassie shouted. "Are you trying to get us all killed?" Then she remembered the incontestable fact that those two were already dead, and amended, "Are you trying to get Lord Royce and me killed?"

"Certainly not, fair lady!" answered Sir Belvedere.

"Do not worry, Cassie," added Louisa. "We have a plan."

That was what Cassie was worried about, them and their *plans*. She retreated back into the carriage, where Lord Royce had already stripped off his coat in preparation of trying to take back control of the carriage.

Cassie allowed herself one instant of watching him appreciatively, then said, "I do not think you will have to perform any death-defying heroics today. It is only Louisa and Sir Belvedere playing some sort of joke. They say they have a plan."

He frowned fiercely. "*Ghosts*? Ghosts are absconding with this carriage?"

She nodded, feeling suddenly very tired after her great rush of fear. "I am afraid so."

He pushed past her to look out the window.

"Good evening, my lord!" Cassie heard Louisa and Sir Belvedere chorus.

Then Lord Royce—looking much more like Phillip again—came back inside, and sat down beside Cassie quietly.

"So they *are* real," he said.

Cassie nodded sympathetically, remembering how bewildered she had been the first time she woke up to find Louisa at her bedside. "Yes. Did you think that they were just a dream?"

Phillip gave a short little bark of laughter. "*Hoped* they were, perhaps. It is never easy to admit that one is wrong."

"No, it never is." She knew *that* all too well.

"But what do they want of us?" he said in an unsettled tone.

"I'm not sure. Just for us to be their friends, I suppose, and help them to understand. They are just as confused about why they are here as we are." She paused for a moment, then went on, "I have no idea why they would want to push us into a runaway carriage, though. That seems mean, and they are not *mean* at all."

Phillip still seemed unnaturally still and calm, as if stunned by the proceedings. "You have talked with them a great deal?"

"We have become friends. I do not know this Lady Lettice at all, though, having just met her last night. Perhaps this was all her idea."

"You must think me a terribly stubborn fool, Miss Richards," he said, raising his gaze to meet hers at last. "For denying all this so strenuously and for so long."

"Stubborn, perhaps," Cassie answered slowly, with the realization that this was a great turning point for him and for *them* as well. A Lord Royce willing to admit he might share his house and now his carriage with some long-dead ancestors was a momentous thing.

The least she could do was not crow in triumph.

"But not a fool," she went on. "This is all very hard for anyone to understand, especially someone who has devoted their life to history and philosophy. I, myself, do not fully understand it at all, and I doubt I ever will."

Phillip took her gloved hand in his and lifted it to his lips for a warm, lingering kiss. "Thank you, Cassandra. For not thinking me *too* great a fool."

She smiled at him. "Did you not tell me that my name means 'disbelieved by men'?"

He laughed against her fingers, and it echoed sweetly to the very heart of her. Cassie leaned toward him, drawn to him by an inexorable force . . .

But then there was a great jolt, and the carriage was thrown off balance. Cassie slid against the leather-padded wall, still holding onto Phillip, who fell heavily against her.

"Oof!" she gasped as the carriage ground to a halt, still askew.

Phillip pulled himself away from her. "Cassandra! Are you hurt?"

She was just breathless and a bit sore where her shoulder had landed against the wall. But she *so* wished he would come closer to her again!

"Not at all," she answered, letting him help her up. "But what has happened?"

"I'm not sure." Phillip pushed the door open and climbed down into the road. "It appears your friends have gone, though."

Cassie clambered after him and looked up to the box to see that he was absolutely right. Louisa and Sir Belvedere had vanished, leaving them all alone on a deserted stretch of road with a lopsided vehicle and winded horses.

No one had ever told her ghosts were so unreliable! They had probably floated right back to the East Tower, where they were warm and cozy.

Cassie pulled her cloak closer around her and turned back to see Phillip kneeling down in the road, examining the carriage wheel. "It appears that this wheel is stuck in a rut," he said.

"Can you loose it?"

"Not by myself." He looked up at her and grinned. "I'm just a weak scholar, you know."

Cassie gave a disbelieving little snort. She remembered the lean, strong feel of his body as he fell against her. "I am sure somebody will come along and find us soon. Surely the others will have followed us."

"No doubt. We can start walking back toward the castle, and meet them on the way."

"Yes, a fine idea." Maybe walking would keep her warm, she reflected, even though her thin evening slippers were hardly made for the road.

Phillip reached back into the carriage to retrieve his coat, slid it over his shoulders, then offered her his arm. "Shall we?"

"Thank you," Cassie said. She took his arm and off they went, as if for a pleasant afternoon's stroll.

But they had not gone far before Cassie realized just how impractical her shoes were. She stumbled over a stone in the road.

"What is it?" Phillip asked in concern.

"Oh, these silly shoes! They are supposed to be able to dance all night, but they cannot walk down a simple country lane." Leaning on him, she lifted up her foot and peered wryly down at the thin blue satin. What she wouldn't give for a nice, sturdy pair of boots right now!

With no warning, Phillip reached down behind her knees and swept her up into his arms. He continued walking down the road as if she weighed no more than a quill pen.

"What are you doing?" Cassie cried, twisting about to look at him.

"Carrying you, of course," he answered matter-of-factly. "You are obviously in no condition to be

walking. Stop wriggling about so, or I'll have to
drop you."

Cassie immediately stilled—and realized how very
nice it was to be held so. His arms were strong and
secure about her, his warm breath stirring in her hair.
She leaned her head against his shoulder, and just
gave herself over to those lovely feelings.

He hummed a soft little tune as he walked. "You
seem quite contented," she commented, marveling at
how this seemingly happy-go-lucky man had been
so quiet and angry only hours before.

"Oh, I am," he answered, shifting her slightly in
his arms. "Just think of all the marvelous new ave-
nues of philosophy that are open to my study now!
That is something to look forward to. Best of all, I
have a very pretty girl in my arms, and I am strolling
along in the evening air rather than sitting at some
dull supper party. Do you not agree that this is more
fun than being at Lady Paige's house, as worthy as
that lady is?"

Cassie thought this was more fun than anything
she had ever done before. She was cold and her feet
hurt, but she wanted to giggle giddily. What a very
good thing it was that the ghosts were so fond of
mischief!

"Oh, yes," she agreed. "Much better."

"You do realize, of course, that I have hopelessly
compromised you," he said in a genial tone.

Cassie's eyes flew wide open, and she stared up
at him. He just smiled blandly back at her.

Was this what it felt like to be compromised? If so,
it was not too bad, though perhaps not *quite* as exciting as one would have imagined. "Have you
indeed?"

"Oh, yes. I shall probably have to marry you." He
sounded singularly unconcerned by the prospect.

Cassie felt an undeniable thrill at the thought of marrying Phillip. But at the same time she felt a stubborn niggling of doubt. She had always fantasized that she would marry for love, as her parents had. She had a sneaking suspicion that she *did* love Phillip, or at least was beginning to.

But did he love her? She rather doubted it. He probably still thought her a silly, flighty girl.

She wanted him to truly *want* to marry her. Not *have* to marry her because the ghosts had pulled a prank for some reason.

And, if they were to wed, she would have to give up any idea of ever going back to Jamaica. Only true love could make her give that up.

She made herself laugh lightly and said, "I hardly think it will come to that! Only my aunt, your mother, and Antoinette know we are out here alone. They will not gossip about it, surely, and the ghosts cannot. They are never invited to dine anywhere."

"Oh, you never know about my mother. She has been so eager to get me married off, she may even be willing to cause a scandal to do it."

Cassie peered up at him suspiciously, not sure if he was joking or not. She had never known anyone with such a *dry* sense of humor before.

He just had that same little, maddening half smile on his face.

"But you needn't fear being leg-shackled to me just yet," he said. "I think I hear a carriage. We are rescued."

Indeed they were. The first carriage from Royce Castle, the one that had *not* run away, rounded a bend in the road just ahead and came barreling toward them, driven by a human coachman. Antoinette, Lady Royce, and Chat all hung out of the windows, the wind disarranging their careful coiffures.

"There they are!" Antoinette shouted, and the carriage pulled to a halt. The women tumbled out and ran across the road to them.

"Cassie!" Aunt Chat cried out. "Are you hurt, my dear? What has happened?"

Lady Royce, too, expressed her concern, but Antoinette looked suspiciously sanguine as she took in the scene of Cassie in Lord Royce's arms.

He slowly lowered her to the ground, still holding onto her arm.

"I am not hurt at all, Aunt Chat," Cassie assured her. "But, oh, you will not believe what has happened!"

For a man whose entire worldview had been turned tip over tail, Phillip was feeling strangely jolly.

They were all crowded into the one carriage now, on their way to Lady Paige's supper at last. Cassie sat beside him, wedged against him as she and Antoinette tried to fix each other's hair into some semblance of tidiness. Even after traipsing about outdoors, her sweet, exotic perfume was still discernible, and she occasionally fell against him as the carriage bounced along the road. She would smile up at him apologetically, then go back to assuring her aunt that no, she was not injured, and yes, she did feel up to going to the supper party.

Her gaze would sometimes meet his, with a little puzzled frown on her brow, but then she would quickly look away. It was clear that his earlier words about being compromised and having to marry were still on her mind. And not necessarily in a good way.

He had tried to convince her he was merely joking when he said that—he tried to convince *himself* he was merely joking. But the truth was he wouldn't half mind marrying Cassandra Richards.

He wouldn't half mind it at all.

He looked down at the top of her dark, shining hair. She laughed at something Antoinette said, and her head tilted back onto his shoulder for the merest second. Her long sapphire drop earrings shimmered in the light from the carriage lamps, then lay still against her white neck.

She was truly the first woman who the thought of marrying did not fill him with some sense of dread. Rather, it filled him with a sense of—anticipation and warmth.

He finally acknowledged to himself that, yes, he was very fond of Cassandra Richards. In fact, he could very well be falling in love with her.

When she first came to Royce Castle, full of fancy and island exoticism, he had been drawn to her, but not at all sure of her. Now he knew that not only was she pretty and vivacious, but she was smart, and caring, and kind to everyone around her.

Even to stubborn old homebodies like himself.

She was also full of life, and she spread that joy in living all about her. He had not realized just how dull and dusty his life had become until she burst into it. Now he never wanted to give up that feeling of being gloriously alive.

He never wanted to give *her* up.

But it was obvious that she could never be happy with the sort of life he could give her, the sort of person he was.

If there was only some way to persuade her otherwise . . .

"Are *you* quite all right, dear?" his mother said, breaking into his thoughts. "You have been very quiet, and you are rather pale."

He looked back down at Cassie, who now watched

him worriedly. "I am quite all right, Mother," he answered. "Quite all right indeed."

"Oh, that was truly splendid!" Lady Lettice said happily as the ghosts gathered in the East Tower to gloat over the evening's triumph. She clapped her beringed hands as she floated over the floor, her skirts barely brushing the carpet. "I must say I had my doubts about the two of you managing things with the carriage, but you did a fine job."

Louisa bristled indignantly. "What do you mean, you had your *doubts*? This entire thing was our doing, Sir Belvedere's and mine. All you did was give Lord Royce that tiny little push into the carriage."

Lady Lettice planted her hands on her hips. "I was the one who orchestrated the entire thing! You would never have even tried it if not for me. Apparently, all the two of you have been doing in the years of my absence is playing chess and pulling tricks on Lord Royce. Very childish!"

If Louisa had not been a ghost, and therefore pale by nature, her face would have flamed with indignation. "I beg your pardon, lady high-and-mighty, but it was *my* idea. . . ."

"Dear ladies, please!" Sir Belvedere interrupted, stepping between them with a loud clatter, as Angelo laughed in delight at the blossoming quarrel. "We all worked on this scheme, and the triumph belongs to all of us. We must concentrate on Lord Royce and Miss Richards, and not squabble among ourselves. Or all our effort will be for naught."

"You are right, of course, Sir Belvedere," Lady Lettice said slowly. Then she went and sat down in the chair beside the window.

Louisa nodded. Sir Belvedere *was* completely right.

They were dead, after all; their troubles should all be behind them, along with human pettiness. This was all about Lord Royce and Cassie, and helping them to not make the mistakes in life that the ghosts had. Cassie had been so very kind to them, so helpful, that it was only right that they should help her in return.

And *someone* deserved to be happy as Lady Royce in this place, even if that someone had never been Louisa.

Chapter Seventeen

"Psst! Cassie! Are you awake?"

Cassie vaguely heard Antoinette's whispering voice through the haze of sleep. She was still muzzy-headed from the wine at Lady Paige's supper, and from the strange excitement of being carried down the road in Phillip's arms. It felt like she had only just fallen asleep, and now here was Antoinette hissing in her ear and poking at her shoulder.

She rolled over and opened one eye to peer up at Antoinette's silhouette in the darkness. "What is it? It cannot be time to get up. It's still dark outside."

"I just realized I left something in the tunnel last night when we were summoning Lady Lettice," Antoinette said. "I cannot sleep for thinking about it. I just wanted to see if you would go with me to fetch it."

"Now? It's been there all this time. Can't it stay just a little longer, until morning?"

Antoinette shook her head. She wore no cap, and her long, thick mane of hair undulated in the shadows. "No, I really think I should fetch it now."

"Why do I have to go with you?"

"Because I don't want to go alone!" Antoinette burst out.

Cassie sat up at that. "You are *scared*," she said, amazed. She had always thought Antoinette could not be frightened of anything.

"I am not scared," Antoinette protested. "Merely— wary. I saw just how mischievous those ghosts can be tonight, when they took off with you in that carriage."

"They meant no real harm. I think they must get bored, stuck here in the castle all the time."

"Well, I don't want to be walking about by myself in the dark, anyway."

"All right, then, I will go with you. If I can come right back to bed after. I have had enough excitement for one night."

So Cassie found herself leaving her snug, warm room in the middle of the night, following Antoinette down the cliff steps to the shore. The pale silver moon was half-obscured by clouds, sending a diffuse, mysterious light across the sky. It was chilly out, but still, with no wind stirring.

She looked up at the moon and the stars, and thought how romantic it all was. How lovely it would be if Phillip was here, with his arms around her. Perhaps he would even kiss her . . .

"No!" she whispered, shaking her head to try to clear it of such silly thoughts. It was only the beauty of the night making her feel all romantical again. If he had not kissed her as they walked alone down the deserted lane, he never would. "I will not think of that right now."

Antoinette, several steps ahead, stopped and looked back at her. "Did you say something, Cassie?"

"No. Must be the wind," Cassie answered.

"Hmm." Antoinette walked on.

Cassie waited at the mouth of the tunnel while Antoinette went in and found her lost item. There were rustlings and knockings, and it was several moments before she emerged again, a small muslin packet clutched in her hand.

"All right, I have it now," Antoinette said. "You can go back to your bed."

"Thank goodness!" Cassie said, pulling her cloak hood up. The night, so romantic only moments before, now seemed just cold and rather lonely.

But when they emerged into the moonlight, they found they were no longer alone. Lady Lettice stood on the shore, staring out over the purple-black sea. Angelo, her little dwarf, sat on a large rock nearby, drawing designs in the pebbly sand with a long stick.

Cassie was caught by the sadness on Lady Lettice's pale face. No wonder the night had suddenly turned so melancholy!

"Good evening, Lady Lettice, Angelo," Antoinette said softly.

Lady Lettice looked over at them and gave a little smile. "Good evening." Her gaze dropped to the little packet Antoinette held. "Is that part of the—apparatus you used to summon me here, Miss Duvall?"

"Yes," Antoinette answered, tucking the packet away inside her robes. "I am sorry if you are unhappy here. I could try to send you back, if you like."

Lady Lettice waved her hand in a dismissive little gesture. "It is of no matter. I like it here as well as I did there, in that strange little sitting room. I just went out for a walk, to think about some things without Louisa and Sir Belvedere yammering at me."

Antoinette walked toward Lady Lettice, the scared young woman who came to Cassie's room gone and the Yaumumi priestess in her place. Cassie followed slowly, warily watching the supposedly harmless Angelo. But he paid no attention to her at all, just went on pulling his stick through the sand and muttering something about spiced wine and roast beef.

"What are you thinking about, Lady Lettice?" Antoinette asked.

"Nothing of any import," Lady Lettice replied in a don't-be-impertinent tone of voice.

"She is thinking about Jean-Pierre," Angelo piped up.

"Indeed? Jean-Pierre?" said Antoinette. "Is he the reason we had to look for you in the tunnel and not in the castle? Is Jean-Pierre in the tunnels?"

"Of course not! Jean-Pierre is not anywhere. I have looked and looked . . ." Then Lady Lettice seemed to realize what she was saying and snapped her mouth shut. Her lips formed a thin little line.

Cassie stared at her, feeling the night become even colder around her. So Lady Lettice had been thwarted in love, just as Louisa had. It was all too sad.

Lady Lettice looked down at them, her head tilted back haughtily. Cassie did not feel as comfortable with her as she did with Louisa. Lady Lettice seemed proud and reserved, not fun-loving and chatty as Louisa was. But now Cassie could see the lurking sadness in her eyes, and she felt sorry for her.

Finally, Lady Lettice looked away from them and said, "Oh, very well. I may as well tell you the tale. Jean-Pierre has been dead for centuries. And so have I, I suppose!" she added with a brittle laugh.

Cassie settled down on the rock next to Angelo to listen to her tale. This was even better than a novel!

"Jean-Pierre was a French nobleman, attached to the retinue of the Duc d'Alencon when he came to England to woo Queen Elizabeth. We sat next to each other often at banquets, and danced, and walked in the gardens." Lady Lettice's harsh features softened as she talked, absorbed in her memories. "He was so very handsome. So witty and so accomplished!"

"So perfidious," Angelo added softly, his eyes flashing.

Lady Lettice shot him a harsh glare. "Hush, Angelo! How was I to know that at the time? He said he loved me, and I was a silly young girl. I believed him."

"What happened then?" Cassie asked.

"I received word that my father was very ill, perhaps dying. I left the Court and came back here to Royce Castle to nurse him. A few weeks later, I had a message from Jean-Pierre, saying he had come to Cornwall and could I meet him in the tunnels. They had not been filled in at all then, and were much larger." Lady Lettice's voice became rushed then, as if she wanted to speed quickly through the rest of her tale and downplay the end of it. "Of course I met him. But I thought it odd that he would not come to the castle; he would only meet me here. Later, I discovered why."

"Why?" Cassie breathed, deeply in suspense.

Lady Lettice's hands nervously toyed with the fan at her belt. "He had stupidly become involved in a plot against the Queen. He needed to escape, to return to France, and he needed me to help him. That was all he wanted of me."

It was very clear how pained this proud lady was to admit such a thing, even hundreds of years after it happened. She would not look at them, just stared out to sea. Angelo slid off his rock and hurried over to her, slipping his arms around her waist for a comforting hug. She laid her hand gently atop his head.

"And did you help him?" Antoinette asked quietly.

"Of course not!" Lady Lettice snapped. "How could I have? I was loyal to the Queen. He somehow found a way and left on his own. I never saw him again, not in the years left of my life and not in the centuries since." She looked down at Angelo and said, almost to herself, "And the moldwort did not even ask me to go with him."

Cassie, suddenly cold again, closed her eyes, and wondered if there was some sort of a curse on this place that made love turn sour.

Well, if there *was* such a curse, Cassie was very determined not to fall victim to it!

Chapter Eighteen

"Oh, this *is* a splendid tale!" Cassie enthused, turning over a page in the volume of *The Iliad* she was reading. The morning sun fell from the library windows across the illustrations, making the ancient mayhem and blood seem to come alive. And the bright light made last night, and Lady Lettice's sad tale, seem nothing but a strange dream. "I don't know why I have never read it before."

Phillip looked up from his own work and smiled at her. They seemed in a great accord this morning, Cassie thought, each of them engrossed in their books, but always aware of each other's presence. It felt—comfortable, cozy. *Right*. It seemed that with the adventure of the runaway carriage things had fallen into place for them.

She wished the morning could just go on and on forever. She smiled back at him happily.

"It is a splendid tale," he agreed. "One of my favorites. Though I would have thought it rather bloodthirsty in parts for a lady's taste."

"Oh, it is the people I find most interesting," Cassie said. "Though the battle scenes do have their own, er, charm about them. Achilles, Agamemnon, Helen, Athena—they are all so flawed, but so great. As all true heroes are."

"And Cassandra? How do you find her?"

"Poor Cassandra! To be so cursed, and all because of a man's treachery. Apollo was terribly fickle, was he not?" Just like Lady Lettice's Jean-Pierre and Louisa's husband, she reflected.

Phillip laughed. "I suppose he was, a bit."

"More than a bit. It must have been terrible for Cassandra, to always know what was going to happen and yet have no one believe her." Cassie wondered if she should tell him about her and Antoinette's midnight encounter with Lady Lettice, but then decided to take a lesson from the Trojan Cassandra and keep silent. He claimed to believe her now, but it was early days yet. Their new accord was still too fresh.

Later, she would tell him. There would be plenty of time later. Right now she just wanted to be happy. In the bright day, her nighttime fancies of cursed love seemed silly in the extreme.

She looked back down at her book, but had only been reading for a few minutes when Phillip said, "Do you like it here at Royce Castle, Cassandra?"

He sounded so uncharacteristically uncertain that she looked up at him in surprise. "Like it here?"

"Yes. Do you feel—comfortable here? As if you could stay for a while?"

Cassie wondered what it was he was asking. He could not be trying to find out if she would like to be mistress of Royce Castle! Could he?

And what would she say, if that *was* what he was asking?

She felt very confused.

"I am sure Aunt Chat would be happy to extend

our visit here, if your mother was to invite us," she answered carefully.

Phillip took off his reading spectacles, and rubbed at the bridge of his nose. "Cassandra, about yesterday evening . . ." he began.

But he did not finish. Antoinette burst through the library door, her expression flushed and startled. "Oh, Cassie!" she cried. "You must come now, at once!"

Cassie looked at her in bewilderment, her mind momentarily unable to make the switch from Phillip's puzzling words to Antoinette's frantic and mysterious summons. "What is it?" she asked.

"A caller has arrived."

"Who? Someone for Lady Royce?"

"Oh, no. Someone for *you.* You will never guess who it is!"

Cassie glanced at Phillip, who, self-possessed once again, replaced his spectacles and said calmly, "Go on, Miss Richards. Our conversation can wait."

She nodded, marked her place in her book, and left the library with Antoinette.

"A caller for *me?*" she said, still confused. It seemed she was nearly always confused since coming to Royce Castle.

Antoinette just hurried off down the corridor, forcing Cassie to almost run to keep up with her. When they reached the drawing room, Antoinette opened the door and practically pushed Cassie inside.

Cassie took one look and froze with shock. Sitting there, chatting with Lady Royce and Aunt Chat, was Mr. Paul Bates, her erstwhile suitor from Jamaica. The one who had come to the docks to propose to her one last time before she set sail for England.

When he saw her, a wide grin spread across his sun-browned face, and he came over to take her suddenly cold hands into his.

"My dear Miss Richards!" he said fondly, lifting her frozen fingers to his lips. "My very dear Miss Richards! How splendid to see you again."

As Cassie looked up at his familiar face, the face she had seen so often across a card table or a dance floor in Jamaica, all of her old life came rushing back to her. For one moment, it was as if no time had passed at all. She had never come to England, to Royce Castle, had never met Phillip. She was just Miss Richards of Fair Winds Plantation again.

Oh, dear heaven! Phillip. They were just becoming so close. What would this look like to him, an old suitor suddenly appearing from across the ocean? Would it look like she did not care for Phillip at all, that she had been pining for Mr. Bates all this time?

"Mr. Bates," she managed to whisper. "Whatever are you doing here?"

"Cassie!" Aunt Chat said with a strained little laugh. "What a way to greet someone who has come such a long way to see you."

"Of course not," Cassie answered politely. "It is very good to see someone from home, Mr. Bates. Very good indeed."

She peered closer at him. He *was* rather handsome; she had forgotten that in the months she had been in England. He was tall, broad-shouldered, with very blue eyes and sun-streaked blond hair. She had enjoyed flirting with him and talking to him when they were neighbors in Jamaica. It was nice to see him again, to remember that old life.

But she also remembered exactly why it was she had turned down his offer of marriage, even when it would have solved many of her troubles and allowed her to stay in Jamaica. She felt nothing when she looked at him, when he took her hand. She felt no warmth, no quick tingle of excitement, as she did when she was with Phillip.

And *why* was Mr. Bates here at all? They had never been such good friends as all that, and her refusal at the docks had been decisive. She had not received so much as a letter from him since, though she had corresponded once or twice with his sister, her friend Mrs. Bishop. There was absolutely no reason for him to have undertaken such a long, deeply inconvenient journey.

Was there?

"Mr. Bates. Why are you here?" she repeated quietly.

He shrugged and gave one of his hearty laughs. But she thought she detected a flash of irritation in his expression, before he covered it in joviality. "I haven't been to England in years! Thought I should come and visit my grandfather in London. The old fellow can't have much longer to go, y'know, and he's quite flush in the pockets. My sister told me you're living in Bath now, so I thought I'd just pop over and say hello to an old friend."

"I'm not in Bath right now," Cassie said, pointing out the obvious.

"The housekeeper at Lady Willowby's house told us we could find you here," a languid male voice said from over by the fireplace. "Paul said we couldn't possibly leave England without seeing you, so here we came."

Cassie peered past Mr. Bates to see a young man lolling on the settee there, a veritable tulip of fashion in a pink coat and primrose waistcoat. She recognized Mr. Albert Morland, Mr. Bates' cousin, who had been generally acknowledged to be the most useless man in Jamaica. All he had ever cared about was rum and wagering and fashion. Now here he was, being equally useless in England.

She sighed, feeling the idyll of these last few days at Royce Castle slipping further away by the second.

She dreaded having Phillip meet these men. Seeing these people from her past, one of them an old suitor, might make him think she did not care for him. When she *did* care, so very much.

But she could not think of that just yet. She had to be polite.

Her smile felt brittle on her lips as she turned to Mr. Bates' cousin. "Mr. Morland. Here you are, too. Why, I would almost think myself home again."

"How do you do, dear lady?" he drawled. "You are looking as lovely as ever. This dreadful cold climate obviously agrees with you." He came over to her and bowed politely over her hand.

"Thank you," she replied.

"And looking as—democratic as ever," Mr. Bates said, giving a disapproving look toward Antoinette, who still stood beside the door. She looked steadily back at him with narrowed ebony eyes.

His gaze fell away, but he went on in a discontented mutter, "Not very many would allow their maids to come into the drawing room and mingle with guests."

Antoinette whirled about and left the room in a flurry of emerald-green robes.

Cassie gave him a cold glare. Her discomfort and confusion gave way to sheer dislike and anger. "Miss Duvall is not my maid, Mr. Bates, as you well know." She walked over and sat down beside her aunt, leaving Mr. Bates standing in the middle of the room.

Mr. Morland snickered, and Mr. Bates' blue eyes flashed with anger, though his careful smile stayed in place. He came and sat down in a chair next to Lady Royce, who was watching the entire proceedings with a distinctly uncertain air.

"How long are you planning to stay in England, Mr. Bates?" Cassie asked.

"We had planned to return to London immediately after we saw you," Mr. Bates answered. "But your good hostess, Lady Royce, has invited us to stay for a masked ball. Is that not kind of her? We will have plenty of time to reminisce about our long friendship."

Cassie was aghast, but she struggled to cover it with an expression of polite blandness. The masked ball was still five days away! And Mr. Bates and Mr. Morland were going to stay for that whole time?

She would never find any more time to spend with Phillip.

"I thought you would enjoy that, my dear Miss Richards," Lady Royce said uncertainly. "It will give you more time with your friends, and allow them to see your charming shepherdess costume."

Cassie smiled at her. Lady Royce was a dear, considerate woman. It was not her fault that Cassie was only just remembering how much she had disliked some of the people she had known in Jamaica.

She remembered the conversation she and Antoinette had had about "planter sorts" when they first arrived at Royce Castle, and almost laughed aloud.

Laughed bitterly, for it had been funny when she had thought herself done with planters forever. It was not so funny now that there was one here before her.

"Of course, Lady Royce," she said. "It was very kind of you. Now, is there any tea left in that pot? I would dearly love a cup."

They went on conversing for another half hour, time Cassie filled with questions about friends and acquaintances, about the family who had bought most of her father's land, and Mrs. Bishop who lived in Negril. Mr. Bates often sent her "meaningful" glances, and she strongly suspected he had some purpose in coming here to see her. A purpose beyond paying respects to a former neighbor.

She did not want to know what that purpose was, did not want to deal with it. Not just now, anyway, while her emotions were in such disarray.

Her suspicions were confirmed when, as they all left the drawing room to change for luncheon, Mr. Bates caught her arm and drew her into a quiet corner of the foyer.

"I must speak with you, Miss Richards," he whispered.

"We *have* been speaking," Cassie said, feigning confusion. She tried to pull her arm from his grasp.

He gave her his condescending "dear little woman" smile, the one she remembered him giving his sister all the time. "We must speak alone. There is something I want to ask you."

Cassie repressed an irritated sigh. She had known this was coming, a renewal of his "suit." Perhaps a few months ago, when she was racked with homesickness, she might have accepted, out of sheer desperation. But not now.

This was her home now, she realized in one flash of consciousness. England was her home. And even if nothing ever happened between Phillip and herself, as she so hoped it would, she would never leave it.

But Mr. Bates *had* come a long way to see her. The least she could do was hear him out.

"Very well," she said. "Meet me in the drawing room this evening. Before supper. We should have a few moments before the others come down."

"Thank you, Miss Richards! You will not be sorry." Mr. Bates lifted her hand to his lips.

They felt dry and cold against her skin. Cassie shivered and pulled away, turning to go up the stairs. As she did so, she saw Phillip, standing silently in the library doorway.

His handsome face was utterly expressionless as he looked at her. Cassie took one step toward him, her mouth open to call his name. But he turned away from her, going back into the library and closing the door quietly.

Dejected, and more confused than ever, Cassie went on up the stairs to the silent haven of her chamber.

"I do not like that Mr. Bates at all," Louisa said, watching out the window of the East Tower as Mr. Bates and his colorful cousin walked about the castle gardens. "Why has he suddenly come here, making calf's eyes at Cassie and throwing all our good work into disarray?"

Lady Lettice, who sat by the empty fireplace grate with a book in her hands, nodded in agreement. She seemed oddly content this morning, not at all her usual acerbic self. Instead, she went about with a serene smile, as if a great weight had been lifted from her. Even Angelo was quieter. He had ceased complaining about food all the time, and now sat on the carpet at Lady Lettice's feet, playing a quiet game of Patience.

"I do not like him, either," Lady Lettice answered. "He seems—desperate. Slippery. He is here for something, *needs* something. And I fear it is not Miss Richards' heart he is after."

"What could it be?"

Lady Lettice shrugged. "Money, mayhaps? He seems just the sort to be a terrible gamester. Is Miss Richards wealthy?"

"I do not know," said Louisa. "She has some lovely clothes and some nice jewelry. I am not sure I would say she is *hugely* wealthy, though. Otherwise why would she live with her aunt and not in her own establishment?"

There was a great knocking and banging on the stairs, and Sir Belvedere emerged through the door. He pushed his visor back and said, "Have you *seen* those dreadful new visitors, my dear ladies? They are not gentlemen at all, I would say. They are assuredly up to something dastardly."

"How do you know?" Louisa asked him. "Did you discover something about them?"

"Not yet. I have not had the time."

"We do not like them, either," said Lady Lettice. She tapped one jewel-bedecked hand thoughtfully on the arm of her chair. "We shall just have to go spy on them! Discover what they are about."

Louisa's eyes sparkled. She truly loved nothing better than a spot of intrigue! "Yes! Let us go right now and search their rooms, while they are out in the garden. Or perhaps we should eavesdrop on them while they are unaware."

So the four of them joined hands and vanished in a flash from the East Tower, only to emerge a moment later behind the tall hedges of the garden maze.

Mr. Bates and Mr. Morland, completely unaware that they were being watched, sat on the marble benches at the center of the maze, placidly smoking and chatting, feeling quite pleased with themselves indeed.

"She is as good as mine, and her land with her," Mr. Bates said, flicking some of his cheroot ashes into the gardener's carefully tended chrysanthemums. "All I have to do is reach out and scoop her up."

Mr. Morland laughed and brushed some imaginary dust from the sleeve of his pink coat. "I must say, Paul, she did not look exactly ecstatic to see you. She didn't run right into your arms, or anything like that. In fact, I thought she was going to faint there for a moment."

Mr. Bates frowned. He had noticed that, as well. "She was just surprised, that is all. She was hardly expecting me, now, was she? She was overcome by the emotion of it." That had to be it, he assured himself. The silly gel had been giddy over him ever since they first met. She was ripe for falling into his arms— for handing over what he wanted.

He conveniently forgot the fact that she had turned down his ardent proposal on the docks in Jamaica and had gotten on the ship without a backward glance. It had just been shock, he thought, and perhaps a belief that he, the most sought-after bachelor of the West Indies, could not possibly be interested in *her*. She was small and dark, and the whole island knew she was a strange one. Look at her friendship with that native woman!

But now he would have to *make* her believe he was attracted to her. His future depended on it.

"She has agreed to see me this evening before supper," he said.

"Indeed?" his cousin drawled. "And what are you going to do? Clasp her in your arms, declare undying devotion? Beg her to elope with you? Say that you will die without her in your life?"

"I will ask her calmly to sell me the land at first. That would be the most sensible thing. And if that does not work . . . I will do whatever will be necessary." Why, he wondered, did upper-class girls have to be such a lot of trouble, anyway?

Mr. Morland shook his head mockingly. "Not your

usual style of wooing at all. Usually you just snatch onto a woman and shout 'Brace yourself, m'dear.' " He had a hearty laugh at his own joke.

Mr. Bates scowled at him. "Well, that's not going to work with this particular female, now is it?"

Mr. Morland slowly sobered. "No. Not if you want to keep your plantation."

"That is the whole reason for this ridiculous excursion! She must agree to give me that land of hers. One way or another."

There was a sudden, sharp rustling in the hedges. Mr. Bates jumped up, looking frantically around. "Who is there?" he shouted. "Show yourself!"

But everything was silent; the only sound was the distant rush of the sea.

"Cousin," Mr. Morland said. "You are growing paranoid. This is not good at all."

"I am *not* paranoid," he murmured, sitting slowly back down on the bench. Yet he could not quite let go of the feeling that *someone* was watching him.

This whole place gave him the shivers and had ever since they first walked in the front door. There was just something not quite right about it.

The sooner he had Miss Richards' land and possibly her person, and they could leave, the better.

Chapter Nineteen

"What do you suppose he wants, then?" Antoinette asked, helping Cassie dress her hair before supper, as Cassie was too nervous to do it herself.

"I have no idea." Cassie was just as puzzled as she had been when she first walked into the drawing room and saw Mr. Bates. She could think of no reason at all for him to come visit her, even if he *was* in England to see his grandfather. She had thought they said everything there was to say that day at the docks.

It was true that she had been rather good friends with his sister, and he had occasionally flirted with her, in a halfhearted way. His behavior had sometimes been flattering, but there was always *something* she could not quite like about him. Something evasive and odd.

That *something* seemed even stronger now than it had then.

For one moment, when she had first seen him, she had let herself indulge in the dream that he had come to declare his love for her, marry her, and take her back to her old life in Jamaica. Was that not what she had wanted ever since she came to England? To go back to Jamaica?

But now she found that that was no longer what she wanted at all. Her life there had been a good one, but it was behind her now.

And, even if it were not, she could not bear the thought of marrying a man like Mr. Bates. Not when she now knew the truth of what a man could be— honest, caring, strong without making others weak, intelligent, and willing to change when situations warranted.

Someone like Phillip.

Phillip, who had seen her in the corridor having her hand kissed by Mr. Bates. And just when things were going so well between them!

She would just have to talk to him, make him understand who Mr. Bates was. But not just yet. First she had to talk to Mr. Bates, and she only had enough strength for one thing at a time.

She reached for the carved ebony comb that had been her mother's, and placed it carefully in the low, braided twist of her hair Antoinette had finished. "Do I look all right?"

"All right for what?" Antoinette asked, peering in the mirror to straighten her own lavender-colored turban. "For running into Mr. Bates' arms and accepting his oh-so-romantic declarations?"

Cassie laughed. "Hardly! I am just praying he makes no declarations whatsoever tonight. I want to find out why he is here and send him on his way as soon as possible."

"On his way—alone?"

"Of course alone! What do you think, that I want to go with him? What fustian!"

Antoinette shrugged. "He would take you back to Jamaica."

"*Nothing* would be worth being married to him. His hands are cold, and his eyes are—are empty."

"Just be careful, Cassie dear," Antoinette said, bending down to give her a quick, reassuring hug. "Are you certain you don't want me to come with you?"

Cassie shook her head, clinging to her friend. "I will only speak with him for a few minutes, and we will be in the drawing room, with the butler within calling distance."

"Very well. I will let you go down alone for a little while, but then I am going to come stand outside the drawing room door until I see him leave."

Cassie laughed. "My dear friend! What would I do without you?" She stood up, and straightened the folds of her emerald-green satin gown. "This will not take long at all, I am sure."

Soon after Cassie left her chamber, Louisa, Lady Lettice, Angelo, and Sir Belvedere appeared there, finding Antoinette alone, trying to read a book and biding her time until she could hurry downstairs.

"Where is Cassie?" Louisa asked.

"She has gone to meet with Mr. Bates," Antoinette answered.

"Oh, no! She cannot be alone with that dreadful man," Sir Belvedere cried. He paced the length of the floor, his armor rattling even more than usual in his agitation.

Lady Lettice said nothing, but twisted one long strand of pearls around her finger nervously.

"I agree that he is truly dreadful," Antoinette said. "But they are hardly alone with all the servants around." Not alone at all, she silently reassured herself.

"Nonetheless, it is not good," said Louisa. "We do not like that man at all."

"He is after Miss Richards' land!" Angelo cried. "Bad, bad man! Angelo hates him."

"Her land?" Antoinette said, puzzled. "She has no—oh, you mean the land she still owns in Jamaica?"

"That must be it. Land in England could scarcely do a planter in Jamaica any good," said Louisa.

Antoinette shook her head. "But it is not a great amount. Cassie sold most of her father's plantation to a new family there. She kept only a plot big enough for a house and a small garden, in case she ever wanted to go back. Of course, it *does* border Mr. Bates' land."

"Then that is it!" Sir Belvedere said. "He wants to marry her to expand his holdings."

"But his own plantation is huge," said Antoinette. "Why would he go to so much trouble for Cassie's piece of land?"

"Greed, my dear lady," Sir Belvedere answered. "Some men will do anything out of greed."

"He is certainly greedy enough," Antoinette agreed. "And the sort of man who will stop at nothing to get what he wants. But what should we do?"

"Just wait," Lady Lettice advised. "Perhaps after Cassandra turns him down he will leave quietly, and we will not have to worry about him anymore."

"What if he does *not* go away?" Louisa murmured.

"Then, Louisa, *he* will be the one to worry about *us.*"

"So who is this Mr. Bates, Mother?" Phillip asked. It was growing darker in the library; he really should have been thinking of going upstairs to change for supper. But all he could keep replaying in his mind was the image of Cassandra standing in the foyer having her hand kissed by some strange man.

A man who was tall, broad, and sun-browned. A man who looked as if he had never spent an hour bent over dusty books in his life. A man who appeared to know her very well.

"He says he knew Miss Richards in Jamaica," his mother said, fussing about with some of the ornaments on the fireplace mantel. She had ostensibly come in to tell him it was nearing time for supper, but as usual she could not resist changing his arrangements about. "He told us he was in England to see his grandfather, and wanted to see Miss Richards before he returned home."

He *would*. "Oh, just happened to be in the neighborhood, eh?"

"I suppose. He seems quite fond of Miss Richards." She gave him a meaningful glance. "I would not be surprised if he was here to ask her to marry him." Then, her point seemingly made, she ceased moving the ornaments and walked to the door. "Supper will be soon, dear. Don't stay here too much longer with your books."

"I won't, Mother," he answered.

As the door shut behind her, he looked back down at the book that lay open beneath his hand. His mother had been repeating that admonition to him for as long as he could remember. "Don't stay up reading too long, Phillip." Even as a child, he had found a new and engrossing world in books, one that was difficult to tear himself away from. It had been the only world he needed.

Until now.

Cassandra had shown him a whole world outside the library, one that was full of color and mystery and light. It was not always neat and rational; it was sometimes messy and unexplainable, and very, very exciting. When he was with her, he felt like anything at all could be possible. He wanted to spend so much more time with her, to learn everything there was to know about her.

And, miracle of miracles, she had seemed to enjoy his company, too.

Until now.

Now there was a man from her home, a home he knew she missed, here to try to reclaim her for that past life.

Phillip laid his hand flat on the crackling pages of the book. Was he back to living only in books, without her color and vividness in his life?

Or could he find it within himself to fight for her?

Mr. Bates was waiting when Cassie slipped into the drawing room. There was a fire in the grate, but the maids had not yet been in to light the candles, so there were shadows lurking in the corners of the room. Mr. Bates almost seemed to be one of them, a large mass in evening clothes outlined by the fire.

"So here you are!" he said with a jovial grin. "I was beginning to think our talk was going to have to take place another time."

Cassie was not put at her ease. His smile seemed too—too forced. She cautiously came farther into the room and sat down on the edge of a chair. "You came so far to see me. The least I could do is meet with you as soon as I could."

"And I am so happy you did." He sat down in the chair beside hers, and Cassie sensed that he would have taken her hand, but she kept them firmly clasped in her lap. "But I did not come all that far. I was already in England, you know, to see my grandfather."

"But he is in London, is he not? That is a great distance from here."

"No distance is too great to see *you*, Miss Richards. Weren't we good friends in Jamaica?"

Cassie would never have gone so far as to say *that*. "Well, I . . ." she began.

He interrupted her by suddenly clasping at the arm of her chair. His rough fingers brushed against the bare skin above her glove and below her short, puffed sleeve, and she drew away from him.

"Of course we were!" he said heartily. "Almost betrothed, some would have said."

No one had ever said that, as far as Cassie knew. "We didn't know each other that well," she managed to say past the growing lump of trepidation in her throat.

"You know I was always fond of you," he said, leaning closer. "That is why I felt I could come to you and ask you something."

"Wh-what?"

"I need to ask you to sell me your land in Jamaica."

Cassie, who had just opened her mouth to refuse a proposal of marriage, looked at him sharply. "My land?"

"Yes. It would be so convenient for me to have it, seeing that it borders my own plantation, and you seem quite settled here."

She almost laughed in profound relief. He did not want *her*—he wanted her land!

But once the relief had passed, questions popped up in her mind. Her land was not very great; it seemed almost as strange that he would come this far to buy it as it had for him to propose to her.

She looked away from him, into the light of the fire. It made sense to sell it to him, certainly. She had no need of it. But something very strong held her back.

That land was her last link to her father. She did not want to let it go to a man who unsettled and alarmed her in such a way.

She turned back to Mr. Bates. He still smiled amiably, but there was such desperation in his eyes. Desperation, and—and something she could not name, but that frightened her.

"I will think about your offer," she said carefully. "But I must tell you I have no plans to sell that land. Not to anyone."

His smile faded, replaced by a puzzled scowl. "You are refusing to sell me the land?"

"I said I would think about it . . ." she began, but her words became a squeak when he suddenly grabbed her arm.

"You also said you have no plans to sell!" he growled. "You were never going to hear me out at all. Just like a woman—stubborn and two-faced! You don't even need that land. You are just keeping it to spite me."

"Let go of me!" Cassie cried, pulling at her arm.

She managed to yank away from him, but part of her sleeve came off with a loud tear. It echoed in the room, and the door was thrown open.

Phillip stood there, tall and still. He frowned as he took in the scene before him, the firelight glinting like the flames of Hades on his dark hair.

"What is the meaning of this?" he said in a frighteningly calm voice.

Cassie gave a small cry and leaped off her chair to run toward him. Never had she been so glad to see anyone in all her life!

He caught her in his arms, and she held tightly to him, trembling and wordless. Usually she felt so confident, so safe in her world; all that had fled before the anger she saw in Mr. Bates' eyes.

But now her world was slowly righting itself as she held onto Phillip.

He looked calmly at Mr. Bates over the top of her head. "I ought to call you out, sir, for frightening a guest in my own home," he said quietly. "As it is, I ask you to leave at once."

Mr. Bates stood up, his polite mask sliding back into place to conceal that quick flash of fury. "You must be Lord Royce."

"I am."

"Well, Lord Royce, Miss Richards and I were just having a bit of a chat about old times in Jamaica. She became rather emotional, as women are wont to do." He gave a jovial between-us-men smile. "You know how women can be. Especially women as—imaginative as Miss Richards. I certainly meant no offense."

"That is not . . ." Cassie began.

Phillip hushed her with a gentle hand on her hair. "I ask you once more to leave my house. I will not ask again."

Mr. Bates drew himself up with a frown and stalked past them to the door. "You will be sorry," he said. Cassie was not sure if he meant her, or Phillip, or the entire world.

As Mr. Bates pushed into the foyer, he nearly knocked Antoinette to the floor. Without even acknowledging her presence, he continued up the staircase.

Antoinette glared at his back, then came on into the drawing room. "Cassie!" she cried. "What has happened? Did that beast hurt you?"

Cassie shook her head mutely. Her voice seemed to have deserted her in the unsettling proceedings.

"I think she is more scared than hurt," Phillip said. "Miss Duvall, would you be so kind as to ask the butler and some of the footmen to make certain Mr. Bates and his cousin leave the castle immediately?"

Antoinette nodded. "Yes, of course! Right away."
She patted Cassie's arm once soothingly and hurried
away to find the servants.

Phillip led Cassie back to the fire and made her sit
down. Then he knelt down beside her, holding her
cold hands in his. "Do you feel up to telling me what
happened, Cassandra?" he asked gently.

"I am not sure," she answered. "It all happened
so very quickly."

A muscle ticked along Phillip's jaw. "He attacked
you?"

"Not *attacked* exactly. He grabbed my arm. But I
had been feeling so very uncomfortable with him,
that when he did that I—I screamed."

"You were very surprised to see him here, then,"
he said, more as a statement than a question. "He
was not an invited caller."

Cassie studied him quizzically. Could that possibly
be a small note of *jealousy* in his voice? That made
her feel slightly better, even in the midst of all her
confusion and fear. Things could not possibly be all
bad if Phillip cared enough to be jealous.

She longed to throw her arms around him and
swear to him that he should never need to feel jealous of anyone. That there was no one in the world
who could possibly compare to him.

Instead, she just nodded her head and said, "Very
surprised indeed. He has never written to me since
I have been in England. I have heard from his sister,
but she has only mentioned him in passing. She did
not even say her brother was coming here." Cassie
paused to take a deep, steadying breath. "I confess I
was a bit glad to see him when first he arrived. He
was a familiar face from home. But I soon realized
that something was amiss. He wants to buy my land
in Jamaica. Very badly."

Phillip, who had been quietly listening and holding her hands, said, "Is there something—special about your land?"

"To me, yes, but surely not to anyone else. It is a small parcel. The only thing I can think of is that it borders Mr. Bates' own plantation, though surely *that* would not have brought him so far to see me. He could have just written with an offer." She shook her head, confused and exhausted, and she could feel the tears starting again. "I just do not know!"

"Sh," Phillip answered. He rose up on his knees and put his arms around her, drawing her close.

Cassie buried her face in the clean, starched scent of his cravat. She had never felt safer or more cherished in all her life.

He rested his cheek against her hair. "You needn't be frightened, my dear Cassandra. No matter what he wants, he cannot get close to you ever again, I promise."

She wound her arms about his neck and held on as if he were the most precious jewel and she feared someone would snatch him away.

Suddenly, the drawing room door was flung open, breaking into the perfect stillness of the moment. Cassie pulled away from Phillip and looked over to see Lady Royce and Aunt Chat watching them with wide, interested eyes.

"Oh! Er . . ." stammered Lady Royce, looking away.

"Perhaps we should go out and come back in again," Aunt Chat suggested.

"Of course not," said Phillip, standing up slowly. His face was utterly expressionless. "Miss Richards has had an unpleasant experience. I'm sure she is very glad to see you."

She *would* have been glad to see them, if only they

had come in just a little later. But she gave them a quavering smile and just said, "Yes, indeed."

Aunt Chat hurried across the room to put her arm around Cassie. "Antoinette told us something of it. My poor dear! Are you quite all right now?"

"That dreadful Mr. Bates," said Lady Royce. She regained her composure and came to take Cassie's other hand in hers. "I cannot believe I let him and his foppish cousin eat some of Cook's best seedcake."

"Now that you are both here, I will just go and make certain Mr. Bates and his cousin are leaving," Phillip said. He bowed to the ladies and went out the door with a resolute set to his shoulders.

"You needn't worry about a thing now, my dear," Lady Royce said, patting Cassie's hand. "My son will take care of everything. That Mr. Bates shall never bother us again!"

Phillip did not bother to knock on Mr. Bates' door. He merely pushed the wood aside and stood in the portal with his arms crossed across his chest.

He did not trust himself to do anything else, such as speak or walk across the room, not with the memory of Cassie's tearstained face in his mind. And anger, sharp and white-hot, unlike anything he had ever felt before, coursed through his veins. If he came within ten feet of Mr. Bates, he knew that he would kill him with his bare hands.

And that would be the height of rudeness, to murder someone beneath his mother's roof.

He stood there, watching Mr. Bates and his cousin as they hurried about the room, tossing things into valises. His expression, his entire being, felt as if it had been turned to stone.

Mr. Bates straightened up from his valise to glare at Phillip, his sun-browned face red.

"The least you could do is send a servant to do the repacking," Mr. Bates said, coming closer to Phillip than was strictly prudent on his part.

Phillip set his jaw. "I fear all the servants are otherwise occupied. Some of the footmen will be here shortly to be certain you depart, though."

"We have never been treated in such a fashion in our lives!" Mr. Bates growled, taking another step closer. "If this is English hospitality . . ."

That did it. Phillip's fragile hold on his temper snapped, and his hands shot out to grab Mr. Bates by his coat front. "How dare you come to my home, uninvited, and insult a young lady in my drawing room? You're a lout and a bully, and I ought to thrash you within an inch of your life." Strength Phillip did not know he possessed flowed into his fists, giving him a viselike grip on the larger man.

Phillip wasn't the only one who was surprised. Mr. Bates' eyes widened, as he struggled to release himself. Behind him, his cousin fluttered about ineffectually, his face pale above his pink coat.

"It—it was not like that," Mr. Bates managed to gasp. "That stupid chit . . ."

Phillip shook Mr. Bates by his coat until the man's head wobbled on his thick neck.

"Phillip!" his mother's shocked voice cried, breaking into his haze of anger.

He glanced back over his shoulder to see her standing in the doorway, her eyes wide.

"Phillip, please," she said quietly. "Come away, now. These—people are not worth it."

Phillip gave Mr. Bates one last shake, and released him. Mr. Bates fell back, trembling. "If you ever come near Miss Richards again, thrash you is exactly what I will do," he warned. "Now, leave my house."

Without another word, he turned, took his mother's arm, and left the room, not even glancing back.

Mr. Bates watched him go with fury blazing in his eyes.

Chapter Twenty

"Well, you certainly made a mess of *that*, cousin," Mr. Morland said, lolling back against the squabs of the carriage as they raced down the road, away from Royce Castle. "Such a wasted journey. We could have been halfway back across the ocean by now!"

Mr. Bates stared fixedly out the carriage window, his sun-browned face red with the force of his anger. His hands clasped and unclasped into fists. "It was not wasted," he growled. "I *will* get what I came here for."

"How? You frightened Miss Richards out of her wits, and we were not even there four hours. You should have listened to me when I tried to give you some advice about wooing a lady. And that Lord Royce will never let you past the gates again!" Mr. Morland gingerly reached up to touch his shoulder, where Lord Royce had grasped it to push him into the carriage.

"I was perhaps too—overeager with Miss Richards," Mr. Bates acknowledged in a grudging tone. "The stupid girl wanted poetry, I suppose, and pretty words instead of plain honesty. But this is not finished, by any means!"

Mr. Morland looked at him curiously. "Do you mean to say that you *told* her what is truly going on? That our grandfather thinks you are an irresponsible lout—which you are—and that your inheritance from him depends on your making a success of your plantation? And that you have gambled away over half your land, and need Miss Richards' property to begin replacing it?"

Mr. Bates glared. "I did not tell her any of that! But if she had just sold me that land, my troubles would be over. I could recoup before the old man finds out anything! He would think I was the most responsible man in the West Indies."

"But Miss Richards will not sell you so much as a blade of grass, especially since you behaved like such a boor."

Mr. Bates' eyes narrowed. "The land will be mine anyway, once she is my wife. And I will not have to pay a farthing for it."

Mr. Morland sat straight up in surprise, forgetting his stylish languor. "Your wife! She is going to marry you?"

"She will, once I put my new plan into action. Listen to this, cousin . . ." He leaned forward and outlined his ideas to the ever-more incredulous Mr. Morland.

Neither of them saw the small, pale figure huddled beneath one of the seats. Angelo clasped his velvet cap over his mouth, giggling merrily in his mind.

Oh, just wait until Lady Lettice hears of this! he thought. He would be set up with sugared almonds for all eternity.

"Are you feeling better, Cassie?" Antoinette asked, putting a tray holding a glass of milk and some biscuits down on Cassie's bedside table.

Cassie leaned back against her pillows and smiled up at Antoinette. She had been trying to find distraction in a new novel, but the events of the evening kept overshadowing the plot of the book, and so she laid it aside.

"I *am* feeling better," she said, reaching for one of the biscuits. "It is good to know that Mr. Bates is gone and we will not see him here again."

Antoinette sat down on the edge of the bed. "I should never have let you go alone to meet with him, no matter what you said. I was not a very good friend."

"No, Antoinette!" Cassie cried. "You are the best of friends. I was simply foolish. I thought I could deal alone with whatever Mr. Bates had to say. Clearly I was wrong."

"And very fortunate that Lord Royce came along when he did."

Cassie smiled at the memory of Phillip appearing in the drawing room, like a knight of old defending his lady fair. "As you say."

Antoinette fell silent, and for a long moment the only sound in the room was the crackling of flames in the grate. Then she said, "What really happened with Mr. Bates, Cassie?"

"I am not exactly sure. He seemed all right at first—friendly, and full of reminiscences about Jamaica. Then I heard what he had really come here for."

"Your land."

"Yes. My land. It would have been the sensible thing to sell it to him, of course. I will not need it. Yet the thought of him owning something that had once been my father's . . ." Cassie shuddered. "It did not seem right. I tried to be diplomatic in my answer, but he became extremely angry very quickly. There was a look in his eyes that frightened me, and when he tore my sleeve I—I screamed. That was when Phillip, I mean Lord Royce, came in."

Antoinette nodded. "It is a very good thing he came when he did."

"Indeed. I would not have thought that Mr. Bates would attack me in the very midst of a crowded house, but I knew from that look in his eyes that he was capable of anything. I do not know why I welcomed him for even a moment!"

Antoinette reached over and squeezed her hand. "Mr. Bates is obviously accustomed to getting what he wants, and he is ruthless." She looked down, a dull red flush spreading across her coffee-colored cheekbones. "Do you remember Henriette, who was a house slave at his plantation?"

"The one who drowned a couple of years ago?"

"There were whispers that it was not an accident."

Cassie frowned. "I do not remember hearing that!"

"Of course you would not have. I heard it among my mother's people. They do not approve of my living with you, but they will still gossip with me. But the point is that I knew of the rumor, and that is why I am at fault for letting you meet with him. I should never have let my distaste for the man keep me from protecting you."

Cassie felt very shaken and fragile. She clung to Antoinette's hand. "I still say it is not your fault at all. Not one whit! He would not have attempted anything here. And besides, he is gone now. Is he not?"

"Yes. He is gone." Antoinette kissed her cheek and stood up. "Drink your milk, now, Cassie, and try to sleep. We are to go have the final fittings on our costumes tomorrow afternoon, and you do not want to look tired and pale for that!" She gave a light laugh that was obviously meant to be reassuring, but was just as obviously false.

Cassie responded with a weak smile and pulled the bedclothes up to her chin. "I promise I will sleep, if you will, too. Good night, Antoinette."

After her friend left, Cassie lay awake, staring out at her firelit chamber. She was *not* afraid of Mr. Bates, not here in Royce Castle, with Phillip and all her friends, both human and spirit, around her. But she did feel very angry that he had come here and disturbed this happy time. He had no right to frighten her and Antoinette, or to come into her life at all.

For this had been a very happy time indeed, she realized, the happiest she had known since coming to England. Maybe the happiest she had known ever. She loved Royce Castle and the wild landscape of Cornwall. She liked having her aunt and her friends all around her, and walking on the shore, and having books to read and horses to ride.

Most of all, she loved being with Phillip. Walking with him, talking to him, and even just sitting in the library being quiet with him filled her with a warm, secure sense of well-being and joy.

When she had first met him, she never would have imagined she could feel this way! She had thought him a stuffy, cynical scholar, nothing like the hearty outdoorsmen she was used to in Jamaica. But now she saw the truth so clearly, both about Phillip and about Mr. Bates and the men like him. *They* had to make the people around them, especially the women, be weak so that they could feel strong. Yet Phillip *was* strong, innately so, and in such a quiet way that he never had to prove with bluster or violence. His kindness—to his mother, his servants, to Antoinette, and to Cassie—was the largest part of that strength.

She did not know why she had not been able to see that from the very beginning.

But she could acknowledge now that she loved him, that there could be no other man like him in all the world. If he could return even a portion of her affection, she could never ask for anything more.

Cassie smiled and closed her eyes, finally feeling that she was at peace and could sleep. She was warm and secure here.

As she was just about to drift into slumber, though, she heard a rattle in the corridor outside her room. Then there was a short silence and another rattle.

She felt no fear; Mr. Bates could not possibly have gotten into the castle. But she did feel quite curious. She slipped out of bed, put on her dressing gown and slippers, and went out into the corridor.

Sir Belvedere was there, marching smartly up and down past her door in his armor. When he saw her, he stopped and gave her a salute.

"Sir Belvedere!" Cassie said quietly, trying not to wake anyone else, though how they could have slept through the rattling was a mystery. "What are you doing?"

"I am guarding your door, fair lady," he answered.

"Guarding my door?"

"In case those Jamaican ruffians return." Sir Belvedere shook his head. "Those two are most untrustworthy, my lady."

"I certainly agree! It is very kind of you to keep a watch for me."

"I am most happy to do it."

"Where are Louisa and Lady Lettice tonight?"

"They are in the East Tower, talking about shoes and jewels. They have been chattering on about them for hours." He pulled a very masculine mystified face. "How can ladies talk about such things as shoes for so long?"

Cassie shrugged. There was just no way to explain to a man, even one who had been dead for five hundred years, the deep fascination a pair of new shoes could hold. "Well, good night, Sir Belvedere. And thank you again."

"You may rest easily, dear lady. I am ever vigilant!" Then he set off on his march again.

Cassie went back into her chamber and crossed the room to close the draperies at the window. A glimpse of a figure in the garden below stopped her, and she paused with her hand on the cool satin.

It was Phillip, standing in the garden within sight of her window, his tall figure limned in silvery moonlight. He waved up at her, and she blew him a kiss, laughing.

She opened up the casement and leaned out to call, "How very secure I will feel tonight, Phillip, with both my window *and* my door guarded!"

He came closer, until he stood just under her window. "Your door?"

"I just found Sir Belvedere marching up and down in the corridor."

"The ghost?" Phillip's tone was rather doubtful.

"He *does* have a sword."

"A real one? Or a phantom one?"

"I have no idea. It looks rather substantial." Cassie feared she was grinning like a simpleton at this silly conversation.

"Well, I just wanted to make sure you were quite all right and that you were able to sleep."

"I was a bit anxious at first," she admitted. "But I feel fine now. Better than fine, in fact. I am sure that I will sleep very well."

"Mr. Bates cannot come back," Phillip said. "There are guards all around the castle."

"I am not afraid," Cassie answered truthfully.

"Good. I would never want you to be afraid."

They watched each other in sweet silence for a moment, a moment that seemed to stretch into eternity yet was over in an instant. Then Phillip smiled and waved at her once more. "Shall we go riding tomorrow after breakfast?"

"Oh, yes. I would like that."

"I would, too. There are some—things I would like to discuss with you. Good night, Cassandra."

"Good night." *My love*, she added silently.

"And you are certain that is what Mr. Bates said?" Lady Lettice asked Angelo, leaning over him intently.

"He is coming back during the masked ball to kidnap Cassie?" Louisa said, appalled.

Angelo nodded firmly, the bells on his cap tinkling. "That is what he told that overdressed cousin of his. His grandfather will take away Mr. Bates' inheritance, which is a very large one, unless Mr. Bates can prove he is a reformed, responsible character by making a success of his plantation. And gambling away a portion of that plantation is decidedly *not* responsible."

"No, indeed," Lady Lettice murmured. "So he wants Cassie's land to begin to replace what he lost."

"He will kidnap her and force her to marry him in order to get it. And to have his revenge on her for refusing him, as well," Angelo said. Then he burst into tears, wiping at his streaming eyes with the velvet sleeve of his doublet. "Angelo doesn't want the evil man to kidnap Cassie!"

"Oh, do cease crying, Angelo," Lady Lettice said. "He will not kidnap her. We will see to that. It was very clever of you to get into the carriage with them."

Angelo sniffled, his tears dissolving into a rather pleased expression. "It was?"

"Indeed it was," Louisa agreed. "Now, it is five days until the masked ball. Plenty of time to come up with a plan of our own." She gave a merry little peal of laughter. "It is certain that Mr. Bates will never darken *our* door again after that night!"

Late that night, when the castle was quiet and dark, Lettice slipped into Antoinette's chamber. She moved quickly and silently, careful not to wake the woman who slept peacefully in the curtained bed. This would be much easier with Antoinette's help, Lettice knew, but she did not want to involve the humans. It could be too dangerous.

She selected one of the leather-bound volumes from Antoinette's bookshelf, and leafed through it until she found what she was looking for. A solidifying spell for spirits.

Lettice smiled as she read it. Sir Belvedere and Louisa were very blithe about the whole matter, not at all considering in practical terms how it might be brought off. But Lettice knew they had to have a plan, and that being able to mingle freely with the humans had to be part of it.

As she read over the spell again, memorizing it, Lettice tried to reassure herself.

"All will be well," she whispered, trying to maintain her hard-won confidence.

Deep inside, though, were the stirrings of doubt and fear. Lettice had not had very many people to care about in all her existence. Just her father, and Angelo, and, for a brief while, Jean-Pierre. Now she had all these fragile humans, who did not even realize the danger they were in.

She never wanted any evil to befall them.

Chapter Twenty-One

It was a bright, cool morning when Cassie and Phillip rode out from the stables and galloped along the cliff-top paths. White-gold sunlight shone down on the blue and foam-white sea below, and a light breeze ruffled the treetops and sent autumn leaves skittering across the path.

Cassie tilted back her head and breathed deeply of the fresh, salty air. She laughed aloud at the glory of the morning.

"You are looking very well today," Phillip commented with a smile.

Cassie gave him an answering grin. "I *feel* well today. And you are looking quite—refreshed yourself."

"Well, I have had a realization of late, and it has lightened my mind considerably."

"A realization?" Cassie thought of her own realizations of the night before. "What, pray tell, was it?"

He just shook his head, and gave her the little half smile she had once disliked so much, but now found adorable. "Shall we walk?" he said, drawing his horse to the side of the path.

"What a good idea. It's such a lovely day." Cassie pulled her own horse to a halt, then waited for Phillip to dismount and come to her assistance.

His hands lingered at her waist as he lowered her to the ground, holding her warm and safe. Cassie leaned against him, her palm laid lightly against his shoulder. His scent of starch and soap and ink was sweet in the cool air.

"So," she whispered, "what was your realization?"

In answer, he shook his head again and took her arm, leading her along the path. The sun was warm on her head, so warm that she took off her hat and carried it in her hand, letting the breeze ruffle her hair.

It *was* a lovely day, and she was content to walk along next to Phillip in silence. The peaceful moments were most welcome after the shock of Mr. Bates' sudden appearance and just as swift exit. Under this sky, with this man beside her, nothing could hurt her.

They walked until they reached a scenic spot overlooking the cliffs and the sea, where there was a weathered old bench. Cassie and Phillip sat down, but he did not remove his hand from her arm.

"So much has happened in the short time you've been at Royce Castle, Cassandra," he said. "More than ever happened in the years before I met you, I vow!"

"Is this your revelation?" Cassie teased. "Never to have houseguests again?"

Phillip laughed. "Or perhaps to have *more* houseguests?"

"Was that it, then? That you ought to expand your social engagements?"

"Something of the sort." His hand slid down her velvet sleeve to her gloved hand, which he held between both of his. "As I said, so many things have happened since you came here. Most of them to the good."

"*Most* of them?"

"Very well, *all* of them. Or almost all. But they have all conspired to make me think. To make me realize that my life of study, while satisfying in many ways, is not enough."

"Is it not?" Cassie said softly, not daring to hope what he might be saying.

"No. I will always love my books and my work, but they are meant to be part of my life, not the whole of it. There must be time for things such as family, and fun, and wonder at the mysteries of life. Things are not always rational—nor should they be."

"You have taught me many things, too!" Cassie said, curling her fingers tighter around his.

"Have I? I've no idea what they could be."

"I have discovered that our lives are *now*. The past is gone from us, and the future unknowable. I loved my life in Jamaica, but it was over when my father died. I could never have it back, no matter what, and I would not choose it if I could. My memories will always be with me, but my home, my life, is here now. I am where I am meant to be." She looked past him, out to where the sea lay blue-gray under the sun. "Life cannot be built on a foundation of all dreams and fancies. There has to be logic and solidity, as well. And family."

"So we have learned from each other," Phillip said thoughtfully.

"I think we have. My time here at Royce Castle has been the best of my life."

"I hope that time is not over yet."

"Of course not. There is still the ball."

"I mean—oh, I am saying this badly. I mean that I hope it will not be over, ever."

Cassie's gaze swung back to him, her hand tightening on his. He watched her seriously, almost warily. "Wh—what do you mean?"

Phillip took a deep breath. "I mean, will you do me the great honor of becoming my wife?"

She stared at him, trying to decide if she had actually heard what she thought she had. Had he actually said those words?

The silence lengthened, and he looked away from her. His hands began to slide from hers, but she grabbed onto them and held them tightly.

"Do you truly want me to marry you?" she whispered.

"More than anything else," he whispered back.

"Then, yes. I will marry you."

"Cassandra!" he said, his voice ringing with triumph. His arms came around her, drawing her against him, and she tilted her face for his kiss.

It was sweet, and ardent, and filled with all the promise of their life to come. All the passion, all the laughter, all the uncertainty—and all the logic, too.

Cassie's hand crept to his cheek, which was warm beneath the thin leather of her glove. The wind blew a lock of his hair loose, and it fell like a piece of silk across her neck.

He drew back, but his arms stayed around her. She rested her head on his shoulder and sighed in contentment. "I thought you would *never* ask," she said.

He laughed, stirring the curls at her temple with his sweet breath. "Never? Dearest, we have only known each other a short time. I moved as quickly as I could."

"But I knew the first time I saw you that I loved you."

"You hated me the first time you saw me!"

She gave a little shrug. "So I mistook one strong emotion for another. I knew I felt *something* for you, something I would not be able to let go of."

"And I knew I felt something for you, as well. Something I could never feel for anyone else."

"Love?"

He paused just an instant too long before saying, "Yes. That must have been it."

Cassie hit him on the arm, laughing. "So sincere you are! Well, no matter what, that is all behind us now. We have found our love, and I am deeply grateful for it."

"As am I. There is just one more detail to decide."

"What is that?"

"When shall we announce our betrothal? At the masked ball?"

"Oh, that would be perfect!" Cassie said in delight. "But . . ."

"But what? You are not changing your mind!"

"Never! I just want to wait until the day of the ball to tell your mother and my aunt."

"Whatever for?"

Cassie was not quite sure, herself. She only knew that she wanted this to be a secret for just a little while longer; she wanted it to be her own happiness. Then, the day of the ball, she would joyfully shout it from the rooftops, and draw everyone else into the pink glow of her contentment.

"I just want to be *quietly* happy about it for a while," she answered. "And your mother is so very busy with the preparations for the ball."

"Hm. You are quite right," Phillip said. "I am sure that the moment she hears the news she will begin planning the wedding. *Two* festive occasions might be too much for her."

"Then we are agreed?"

"Agreed. It will be our secret until the day of the ball."

Then he drew her back into his arms for another kiss, one to seal their betrothal. It was very late indeed when they arrived back at the castle.

"You are getting *married*?" Antoinette cried, staring at Cassie in a stunned manner. "Truly?"

Cassie laughed and tossed her hat and riding crop onto her bed. As soon as they returned from their ride, she had gone to tell Antoinette the news. She might be able to keep a secret from Lady Royce and Aunt Chat for a short time, but she could never keep a secret from Antoinette.

"I am truly getting married," she said. "Are you not happy for me?"

Antoinette finally managed to close her mouth and rushed over to hug Cassie. "I am more than happy for you, my dearest friend! Lord Royce is a good man and deserving of your love." She drew back to peer closely into Cassie's face. "You do love him, don't you?"

"Of course I love him," Cassie said. "I would not marry him otherwise."

"I know you would not. It is just that when we first met him, you were not—overly fond of him."

Cassie smiled at her and went over to the dressing table to let her hair down and start brushing the tangles out. "That was then. And you did not care for him at first, either."

"He has proven himself to be a man of open mind and great intelligence, and not just intelligent from books, either. He has a kind heart, and he loves you a great deal. I could ask for nothing more for you." Antoinette's reflection in the mirror smiled, but her eyes looked sad and distant. She turned away and sat down in a chair beside the fire.

Cassie wanted no sadness from anyone she loved on this day. She wanted everyone to feel as joyful as she did! She put down the brush and swung around to face Antoinette. "Is something amiss? Did something happen while I was gone?" A terrible thought struck her. "Is Mr. Bates . . ."

"No, no!" Antoinette answered quickly. "He has not been seen again. It is just—well, I have been thinking perhaps I should go back to Jamaica. After your wedding would be a good time."

Cassie was absolutely appalled. She ran across the room to kneel down beside Antoinette's chair, and took her friend's hands in hers. "No! You cannot leave me."

"Cassie, you know I would miss you horribly. But you are beginning a new life now, a new circle. Perhaps it is time for me to go back."

Cassie shook her head violently. "You said when we left that there was nothing for you in Jamaica. That your mother's family, well, that they did not . . ." Her voice trailed away.

"That they did not approve of my closeness to a white family," Antoinette finished gently. "No, they did not, and they chose not to let me be a true part of their community any longer. You were all my family, and I was happy to come here with you."

"Are you not content here in England? Do we not have a good life?"

"A very good life, and I am quite content here. I was looking for a new beginning of my own, you know. But we both know that it is highly unlikely I will ever marry. I can't stay under your feet forever."

"You are hardly 'under my feet'!" Cassie protested stubbornly. "I need you. The ghosts need you, and

Aunt Chat needs you. One day, my children will need you. If you grow bored here at the castle, you can always go see Aunt Chat in Bath. But I will *not* hear another word about your returning to Jamaica! And that is that."

Antoinette smiled. "No one could ever argue with you when your mind is made up."

"No, indeed. So, you will stay?"

"I will stay. Only for as long as you need me, though."

"Then you will be here forever!" Cassie cried happily. "Oh, Antoinette! We are going to be so happy here. I can just feel it."

Chapter Twenty-Two

The next few days passed very quickly, in a blur of social engagements and preparations for the masked ball. Under Lady Royce's careful supervision, the ballroom was cleaned and polished from the frescoed ceiling to the parquet floor. Musicians were hired, new draperies were hung at the windows, and potted palms in unheard-of quantities were brought in.

The costumes were delivered by the dressmaker, and tried on amid much laughter and posing. Guests from far away arrived to stay at the castle and at the inn in the village. They were entertained with suppers, and card parties, and picnics on the shore. There was tea at the Lewishams' vicarage, where they were invited to help plan the annual parish bazaar, and a musicale at Lady Paige's house.

With all the activity swirling around them, Cassie and Phillip could not find a great deal of time to spend quietly together. But they would take their books to the garden in the mornings and stroll the paths and talk about their readings. It was all perfectly proper, and if they occasionally crept behind a hedge to exchange a quick, stolen kiss, who was to know?

At night, Cassie would lie in her bed and hug all the warm happiness of the day close to her. She had truly never been more content than she was now at Royce Castle, and every moment was precious to her, a perfect pearl she could take out and marvel over again in the darkness of her room. She was surrounded by friends, by warm security, and the shining promise of love and a good future.

She clung to these things, as if a small part of her feared they might be snatched away.

"You are certain this is what they mean to do, Angelo?" Lady Lettice said, kneeling down to place her hands on the dwarf's small shoulders.

He nodded vehemently. "Very certain! I snuck into their lodgings again tonight. Mr. Bates is very angry. Very angry indeed. He wants revenge on Miss Richards and Lord Royce. Angelo does *not* like him!"

Lady Lettice patted his shoulder and stood up. "We will not have to worry about him at all after tomorrow night. Is everyone ready?"

Louisa and Sir Belvedere nodded.

"Cassie's costume is a shepherdess, which Mr. Bates knows since Lady Royce mentioned it when they first arrived here," said Louisa. "I have discovered she keeps it in the dressmaker's box at the bottom of her wardrobe."

"And I have examined the 'gentlemen's' carriage," said Sir Belvedere. "There will be no trouble at all."

"Excellent," Lady Lettice said with a smile. "Then we need only wait for tomorrow night. When they make their move, we shall make our own."

*   *   *

The day of the masked ball was a cold one, with a gray sky and an angry, frothy sea. This put an end to the planned luncheon picnic, and all the houes-guests at Royce Castle had to stay indoors. There were card games in the drawing room and charades in the gallery. Servants hurried to and fro, carrying costumes to be pressed, trays of tea, and, as the preparations for the ball itself commenced, hot water for baths.

Laughter and chatter echoed through the ancient castle, as they had not for so many years.

Lady Royce went once more to examine the ballroom before she went to dress. It looked as it had when she had first danced there as a young bride, so very long ago. Footmen were lighting candles in the sconces, casting a golden glow over the cream brocade upholstery of the chairs and the deep yellow-green leaves of the palms. The musicians were practicing on their dais, a sweet, old-fashioned minuet.

If she closed her eyes, she could almost imagine herself swirling about the dance floor with her husband again . . .

A gentle hand touched her arm. "Edward," she whispered, without thinking. When she turned around to look, she found not her husband, but her son, who was his very image.

"No, Mother. It is me," Phillip said gently.

She laughed. "Oh! I am very silly. I was thinking of my first ball here. Your father was so very handsome!" She laid her hand against his cheek, and he covered it with his own warm palm. "You look so much like him."

"I miss him, too, Mother," he said. "I remember how much he enjoyed a ball! He would like this tonight."

"Indeed he would. But you are not yet dressed in your costume, dear! We should be getting ready."

"We will, Mother, but I wanted to speak with you about something first."

"Of course. What is it? Is there something you do not like about the arrangements? I know that you prefer your quiet . . ."

"It is not that at all. I am sure the ball will be perfect." He took her arm and led her to some chairs arranged in a quiet corner, out of the way of the hurrying servants. "I have some news for you."

"*Good* news?" she asked worriedly. She wanted nothing to spoil this night.

Phillip laughed. "Of course it is good news! I have spoken to Lady Willowby this afternoon, and have been given 'official' permission to make it public. I asked Cassandra Richards to marry me, and she accepted."

She stared at him in stunned silence. Was her fondest hope, the one she had thought could never come true, happening? Had her son found love?

"You and—and Miss Richards are to be married?" she whispered.

His hopeful smile flickered at her wide-eyed shock. "Yes. I love her, Mother. And, amazingly enough, she returns my feelings. I would like to announce the betrothal tonight at the ball."

Pure, perfect joy, unlike any she had felt since the night of that long-ago ball, burst through her. She flung her arms around him, sobbing against his neck.

"Mother!" he said, startled. "Are you not happy?"

"I am beyond happy! All my prayers are answered, my dear Phillip. I am to have a daughter at last!"

If either of them had looked up to the portrait of Edward Leighton that hung on the wall, they might have noticed a suspicious brightness about the painted blue eyes. But the sparkle turned back to matte emptiness before they even quit laughing.

"What do you think about my new coiffure, Antoinette?" Cassie asked, twisting about to examine her reflection in the dressing table mirror. Long, carefully formed dark curls bounced and danced over her shoulders. "I think it may be a bit—silly."

"Not at all!" Antoinette answered, adjusting her own costume around her tall figure. She was dressed as Cleopatra, in long pleats of white muslin, cinched in at the waist with gold cord and with a collar of turquoise and coral beads over her shoulders. A gold headdress in the shape of a serpent sat atop her upswept hair. She looked exotic and regal. Cassie only wished she had thought of being Cleopatra first. "You are a shepherdess, Cassie. You are meant to look a bit silly."

Cassie *wanted* to be elegant, as Antoinette was. This was not a night for "silly"!

Yet her happiness at the prospect of dancing with Phillip, as well as the announcement he wanted to make, overcame everything. She laughed, gave her curls one last shake, and went to take the dressmaker's box containing her costume out of the wardrobe.

She lifted the lid—and paused, puzzled. "Antoinette."

"Yes?" Antoinette said, fussing with her headdress.

"This is not the costume the dressmaker delivered the other day, is it?"

Antoinette came to peer over her shoulder. "Not at all! You tried it on, remember? It was not like that one bit. Is this a joke?"

"I am not sure." Cassie unfolded the costume in the box. It was assuredly *not* the blue-and-yellow shepherdess dress. The straw, ribbon-trimmed bonnet and the crook were missing, too.

This was a gown in the style of the Restoration era, and, despite its obvious age, it was in beautiful condition. The pale blue satin was whole and unfaded, and the copious ruffles of white lace were only slightly yellowed. All the pearl beadwork on the bodice was intact.

Cassie unfolded it, spreading it over her lap. It was the most beautiful gown she had ever seen.

Antoinette reached out to touch some of the lace. "It looks like one of Louisa's gowns."

"Why would she take my shepherdess costume away and leave this?" Whatever the ghost's strange reasons, though, Cassie was glad she had done it. She would feel like a queen in this glorious satin.

Antoinette shrugged. "Maybe she wishes *she* could dance at the ball tonight. Here, let me help you put it on."

It fit perfectly once Antoinette had tightened Cassie's corset strings. The satin lay smooth against her, the ruffles frothing about her like the foam of the sea.

Cassie took her mother's pearl necklace out of the jewel case and clasped it around her throat. Now she felt absolutely perfect.

"Is it time now, Lady Lettice? Is the ball starting?" Angelo said excitedly, dancing about the East Tower until the bells sewn on his doublet jangled.

"Very nearly." Lettice peered closely at herself in the mirror, straightening her headdress atop her upswept red hair. The solidifying spell had worked beautifully, and Sir Belvedere and Louisa were off on their last-minute errands. Her plan was falling carefully into place. She should be satisfied and excited.

She felt nervous, though, and almost—almost afraid.

Lettice had never been afraid in her life, or her death! But she was now. Fear hovered around the edges of her mind, and caused her high lace ruff to flutter with the force of her trembling.

Angelo paused at her side, peering up at her with his wizened little face. "What is wrong, Lady Lettice?" he asked, tugging at her skirts.

Lettice forced herself to smile carelessly. "Not a thing! Our plan is coming together."

Angelo smiled. "And soon we will be completely rid of Mr. Bates! Angelo can hardly wait."

Neither could Lettice. If she could just as easily rid herself of these fearful premonitions . . .

Chapter Twenty-Three

"Remember, she is dressed as a shepherdess," Mr. Bates hissed. He and his cousin sat in the darkened recesses of their carriage, parked out of sight just inside the gates of Royce Castle.

For the first time, the languid Mr. Morland looked uncertain. He peered out the window as guests' horses and carriages processed through the gates and up the drive. "Will there not be many shepherdesses there? Ladies seem dashed fond of that sort of thing."

"None of them will have hair like hers," Mr. Bates muttered.

"Are you certain this is a good idea, Paul?"

Mr. Bates shot him a glare. "We have no choice! Are you turning coward on me now?"

"Of course not! It is just . . ."

"Just nothing. This is the plan. If you have no stomach for it, you can start walking back to our lodgings. And keep walking all the way to Jamaica. But don't expect to have a home with *me* when you get there."

Mr. Morland lapsed back into silence.

"Right," said Mr. Bates. "Well, I am off, then. You wait here and keep an eye out for my signal."

He drew the hood of his domino up over his head and slipped out of the carriage, blending in with the stream of guests heading toward the castle. Soon, very soon, Miss Richards and Lord Royce would be deeply sorry they had crossed him.

Cassie stood outside the ballroom doors, watching the dancers move through the patterns of the dance. Beneath the rich glow of the lights, they were a blur of many colors and many time periods. There were knights and their damsels, Harlequin and Columbine, Renaissance poets, Lucrezia Borgia, Henry VIII and Anne Boleyn, Aphrodite, Marie Antoinette. And there were also several gentlemen who had obviously thought it beneath their dignity to wear a costume, and had appeared in evening dress and masks.

The rich fabrics and the ladies' jewels shimmered, and champagne sparkled in heavy crystal.

Cassie's foot tapped lightly to the bright music, and she felt a thrill of excitement as she examined the magical scene. It truly looked like a fairyland, an enchanted place. The perfect spot to announce her new happiness to all the world.

If only she could see her would-be betrothed!

She saw Antoinette-Cleopatra talking to the Lewishams over by the window, and Aunt Chat, in her deep green velvet Eleanor of Aquitaine gown, dancing. And Lady Royce was greeting her guests, looking magnificent in black satin and pearls as Queen Elizabeth.

From the corner of her eye, Cassie saw a flash of white. She turned her head to watch as Lady Lettice, with Angelo close behind her, made her majestic way across the room. Obviously other people saw her, too, as they made way for her wide white silk skirts. She paused to speak with a cluster of guests, peering close at their masked faces as they talked. Then she looked at Angelo, shook her head, and continued on to the next group.

Whatever was she about?

Cassie did not have long to puzzle over Lady Lettice, though. A gentle hand touched one of the lace ruffles of her sleeve, and she looked over her shoulder.

"Phillip!" she said happily, putting her arms around him in a quick embrace, after she ascertained that no one was paying any attention to them. "There you are. I couldn't see anyone in there who looked the least bit like you." She stepped back to examine his costume. "But why are you dressed like a monk, of all things?"

His long brown robe covered him from the top of his hooded head to his feet. He glanced quickly around, then whispered, "This is not actually my costume."

Cassie was puzzled. "It isn't? Then why are you wearing it?"

"To cover up my real costume, of course."

"Don't be silly! Let me see it."

"I think I would prefer to wear the robe."

Cassie laughed. "It is absolutely drab! And that fabric is scratchy. How can we dance if you keep scratching me?"

"You are most persuasive, my dear. If I have to take it off in order to dance with you, then I shall." He looked around once more, then loosened his rope belt and pulled the garment off.

Beneath it, he wore the most amazing thing Cassie had ever seen. She clapped her hand to her mouth to hold her giggles in. They would not be contained, though; they burst forth in a merry torrent. "Oh, Phillip! You look—incredible."

His Greek chiton fell in white silk folds almost to his knees and was trimmed in gold embroidery worked in a Greek key pattern, and held in with a gold sash. The gold sandals on his feet laced up to meet the hem. Even behind his gold mask he looked most disgruntled.

"Incredibly foolish, you mean," he muttered, tugging the embroidered hem lower. "I never should have listened to my mother when she suggested I wear a Grecian costume."

"Not foolish at all," Cassie said, going up on tiptoe to kiss his cheek. "You look very handsome. The most handsome gentleman at the ball, I would vow."

He smiled down at her. "And you are the most beautiful lady. This is an exquisite gown. But I thought you were meant to be a shepherdess."

Cassie preened for him in her blue satin. "I was, but someone took that costume and left this in its place."

"Someone?"

"I suspect Louisa. This looks like one of her gowns." She paused, remembering Lady Lettice and Angelo walking about the ballroom. "Speaking of ghosts . . ."

Phillip gave a long-suffering sigh. "What about the ghosts? What mischief have they done now? I swear, my life was far easier before I believed in them."

"They have done no mischief that I know of—yet. But I just saw Lady Lettice and Angelo mingling among the guests. And where they are, Louisa and Sir Belvedere are sure to follow."

Phillip peered past her into the ballroom, his gaze searching through the company. His expression was wary and surprised. "The guests could see them, then?"

Cassie took her white satin half mask out of her

reticule and tied it over her face. "Oh, yes. She was talking to them and everything. You are not angry, are you?"

Phillip laughed. "Of course not! Surprised, perhaps. I find it so strange and amazing that they have been a part of my life all these years and I am only now seeing them. But I would imagine they get rather bored. A masked ball is the perfect opportunity for them to get out; no one will think their clothes odd at all."

"Exactly! I am sure they are up to no mischief at all." But Cassie bit her lip uncertainly.

"I think my mother has seen us. Are you ready to go in?"

"More than ready."

She took his arm, and swept into the ballroom to join the swirl of color, music, and excitement.

Louisa twirled about in the middle of Cassie's bedroom floor, enjoying the way her skirts belled out around her ankles. It had been decades since she had changed her gown, and the shepherdess costume was very different from her usual heavy satin and silk skirts. It was made of light muslin, with a yellow-and-blue-striped skirt, and a bodice and panniers of blue flowers on a yellow background.

She straightened the blue satin bow at the low, square neckline and smoothed the ruffles of the elbow-length sleeves. It was very fortunate that she and Cassie were almost the same size, and that she was able to change clothes at all. She hadn't been certain she could solidify, having never tried it before, but the spell Lady Lettice had taught her worked. But she knew that it would not last long, and that she would be very tired when it was all over.

The dress looked quite fetching, and she was rather fond of the adorable little shepherd's crook, with its cluster of blue and yellow ribbons. But the hair was all wrong. Louisa twisted one of her ringlets around her finger, examining its silvery-blond color. Cassie's hair was as dark as night.

She would just have to try to will it to change. She had never done that before, either. If solidifying would leave her exhausted, she had no idea what a change of hair color would do.

Ah, well. There was only one way to find out. Louisa closed her eyes, clutched the ringlet tightly in her fist, and filled her mind with the color black.

When she opened her eyes, the curl she held out was coal-colored. She pulled the thick mass of her hair over her shoulder, and saw that it had all turned brunette.

"Oh, I *am* good!" she cried, doing a happy little dance.

Lady Lettice came into the room then, opening the door and closing it behind her like a real human being. "Are you ready yet, Louisa? I think . . ." She paused, tilting her head back to examine Louisa. "Oh! You look just like Cassie with that dark hair."

"Thank you," Louisa said, and reached for the yellow half mask with blue ribbons. "Is Mr. Bates here yet?"

"Not at present. I looked at every guest in that ballroom, and none of them looked like Mr. Bates or his cousin. I left Angelo there to keep a sharp eye on things—if he can tear himself away from staring at the refreshments." Lady Lettice peered into the dressing table mirror and straightened her jeweled headdress with its long white and silver veil.

"I am ready," Louisa said, picking up Cassie's bonnet and the shepherd's crook.

"I do hope Mr. Bates appears soon. We can remain in this solid state for only a few hours."

"Oh, we will be done with this business long before that," Louisa answered confidently. "We will even have time for dancing after!"

"That is my costume!" Cassie whispered in Phillip's ear as they waltzed around the dance floor. She looked over his shoulder at the edge of the ballroom, where a slender figure in a blue-and-yellow shepherdess costume stood. The figure waved the crook at Cassie, then turned and disappeared back into the crowd, dark curls bouncing.

"Someone else is wearing your costume?" Phillip asked, spinning her jauntily around a corner.

"The shepherdess one I told you about. I think it is Louisa, but she has black hair now. She looks just like me!"

"Well, people do say imitation is the sincerest form of flattery."

Cassie laughed. "Who says that?"

"I am not sure. I think it was my mother, when she saw Lady Paige wearing a new bonnet in church that was almost exactly like her own."

She glanced once more over at where the shepherdess had stood, but she was quite gone. Cassie still thought it was very odd, but then she smiled up at Phillip and determined to concentrate on him, and him alone, for tonight. After all, this was their magical night, one they would tell their grandchildren about one day.

And it was certainly proving memorable so far. The music, the laughter of the guests, and the wonderful sensation of twirling about in the dance with Phillip, conspired to create a glittering entertainment. Cassie could not seem to cease smiling.

Yes, this was their night. Nothing, not even mischievous ghosts, could ruin it.

Louisa moved through the crowd, reveling in the feeling of being at a ball again. Usually Royce Castle was so quiet, with only the other ghosts for company. In her life, Louisa had been so fond of parties, just like this one. She hummed along with the music as she walked, smiling at the other guests and eyeing the bubbling, golden champagne enviously. But being solid only went so far. It probably did not permit drinking.

Even if it had, she needed to keep her wits about her if she was to foil Mr. Bates' plan. She looked over at Lady Lettice, who shook her head slightly. No, Mr. Bates was not there yet. Then she turned to Sir Belvedere, who was talking with Cassie's aunt. He also shook his head.

Where could the villain be? Louisa frowned. If he did not appear soon, their plan would have to change. They *could* foil him in their usual forms, but it would be harder.

She scanned over the rest of the company, carefully scrutinizing every man's disguise. A cardinal, a Louis XIV, a medieval prince, Shakespeare, a Cavalier . . .

She paused and looked back at that last one. He *was* dressed as a Cavalier from her own lifetime, his blue satin and white lace a perfect coordinate to the gown she had given Cassie. His long, dark hair fell from beneath a wide-brimmed, plumed hat, which concealed his features.

Then he turned his head and looked directly at her.

"No!" Louisa gasped aloud, startling the people who stood beside her. "It cannot be."

She took one step toward him, but he vanished.

And someone grabbed her shoulder from behind, pulling her away from the crowd. She twisted around to look, half-hoping, half-fearing . . .

It was not *him*, though. It was Mr. Bates. He wore a hooded domino, yet it was still easy to see who it was. His eyes burned through the eyeholes of his mask, and his grip on her was strong and angry.

Louisa longed to bash him on the head with her crook, but then she remembered she was meant to be Cassie, who had no idea about this plan. She put a look of confusion on her face and hoped her old skills at amateur theatricals had not left her.

"What is this?" she said softly, with a quiver of fear in her voice. She remembered to keep it pitched low and soft to disguise it. She made her shoulders shake beneath his hands. It should be easy to lull this thickheaded man into thinking he had a poor, weak female in his grasp. He was the sort who always underestimated women. "Who are you?"

"What, Miss Richards? You do not recognize me?" He sneered at her. "I suppose you thought you would never see me again."

"Mr. Bates?" she gasped. "Lord Royce told you never to come back here!"

"That *scholar*? He couldn't stop me, now, could he? Here I am." He laughed, a soft, humorless, chilling sound. Even Louisa, who had nothing to fear from him, shivered. "I see he has abandoned you to waltz with someone else. How ungallant."

"That is a friend of mine he is dancing with! And if you think . . ."

"Hush!" Mr. Bates squeezed her shoulder cruelly, and showed her a glimpse of a gleaming dagger hidden beneath his domino. "Stop chattering, woman. I do not have all night to stand here listening to you. Come along." He slid a hard arm around her waist, and tugged her along the short distance to the French doors leading to the terrace.

Louisa pretended to dig her heels in, while waving her crook in a signal to Lady Lettice and Sir Belvedere. "Where are you going? Do not do this, Mr. Bates, I beg you!"

"Be quiet!" he hissed, pulling her across the terrace and down the stone steps. "You will see soon enough."

Louisa feigned sobbing and protestations, but behind her mask she was secretly smiling. This was all turning out even better than she had hoped!

In all the excitement of her abduction, she quite forgot the Cavalier she had glimpsed so briefly in the ballroom.

Chapter Twenty-Four

Mr. Bates pulled Louisa inexorably along the dark drive, leaving the lights and noise of the ball farther behind with every step. Louisa, though inwardly highly amused by the proceedings, did her very best to appear frightened and unsure. It was not hard to do; in her life, Louisa had been fond of amateur theatricals and had often acted in plays during house parties at Royce Castle. She was just happy to try the skill again.

In that vein, she gave a little whimper and said, "Why are you doing this? I do not understand! I thought we were friends."

His arm tightened on her waist as he half dragged, half carried her across the gravel. "Friends? A *friend* would have sold me the land. A *friend* would not have been so stubborn and unkind."

"Why do you need the land, anyway?" Louisa said, feigning confusion. "It is all I have left in Jamaica, while you possess so very much."

"So you think," he muttered.

"What do you mean?"

"Never mind. Just come along and quit chattering at me. There is the carriage just ahead."

The black, closed vehicle was half-hidden in the shadows at the edge of the drive, just outside the tall gates. A coachman, muffled in a dark cloak and a hat pulled low over his brow, sat on the box.

As they moved closer, the door opened, and Mr. Bates' cousin stuck his head out. "There you are at last! I thought I was going to have to come fetch you. Did you stop to indulge in some of the champagne?" He snickered.

"Very funny indeed. Our little guest here was late coming to the party." Mr. Bates lifted her off her feet and pushed her toward the carriage door.

As he did so, a voice called, "Here! What do you think you're doing?"

Louisa looked over Mr. Bates' shoulder to see a footman running down the drive in their direction. *Oh, how tiresome,* she thought. A rescue attempt would simply ruin everything.

Apparently, Mr. Bates felt the same way. He stuffed her unceremoniously into the carriage, causing her to lose her crook, and climbed in after her. "Drive, blast it!" he shouted at the coachman, and they took off down the lane with a jarring lurch.

Louisa landed atop Mr. Morland, who set her aright with more wandering hands and leering glances than the act strictly required.

Louisa snatched the bonnet off her head and glared at him from behind her mask. He just smirked back at her. She slid into the corner, as far away from him as she could get. Really, he was even more unpleasant than his cabbage-headed cousin.

"So, now that you have me here, what are you going to do with me?" she asked, smoothing her disarranged skirts.

"We are going to Gretna Green, my dear Miss Richards, where we will be married," Mr. Bates answered.

Admittedly, Louisa's geography was a bit rusty, but . . . "Isn't that rather far away?"

"You will be so hopelessly compromised by the time we reach there, that you will be *glad* to marry me," he said. He was obviously trying for an air of confidence, but Louisa sensed the uncertainty in him.

Really, she thought, it was just too easy. If he had succeeded in making off with the real Cassie, there would have been a thousand opportunities for her to escape between here and Scotland. This was not a very well-thought-out plan on Mr. Bates' part.

If there was anything worse than a villain, in Louisa's estimation, it was a stupid villain. It was just a good thing that soon he would be gone from England forever, and would bother no one with his nuisances again.

Except for the poor people of Jamaica, of course.

Louisa peered out the window, wondering idly when Sir Belvedere and Lady Lettice were going to make their appearances. Suddenly, much to her shock, Mr. Bates grabbed her arm and pulled her onto his lap.

"What are you doing?" she screamed as his wet lips found her bare neck. "Let go of me at once!"

"We might as well start the compromising now," he said, reaching for her skirt while his cousin laughed. "Just in case you have any idea of leaving us soon."

Louisa beat him over the head and shoulders with her bonnet. "Release me, you ridiculous looby!"

"Not just yet," he answered.

Absolutely furious, Louisa squeezed her eyes shut and concentrated very, very hard on her hair, and then on her entire body. Gradually, she felt the faint tingling sensation that meant she was moving from her temporary solid form back to her usual insubstantial state.

When Mr. Bates reached one of his meaty hands to her breast, he found no warm, yielding flesh. Only cold air.

He fell forward, his face turning from scarlet with lust to chalk-white with fear. His mouth opened, but no sound emerged. He just sat there, frozen, staring at her.

Mr. Morland edged back along the seat. "What is happening?"

Louisa took off her mask, sending her now-blond curls tumbling about her shoulders, and turned to look at him.

He gasped for air. "You—you are not Miss Richards!"

"Of course I am not. You stupid men snatched the wrong woman. My name is Louisa, but you may call me Lady Royce. You can find my actual self in the family crypt at St. Anne's Church, but I occasionally come back to pay calls on very special people. Like yourselves."

"As do I," said Lady Lettice, appearing on the seat next to Mr. Morland. "How do you do? I am Lady Lettice Leighton. And that is Angelo down there, beneath the seat. The one who is tying your ankles together."

Mr. Morland looked down, and saw that small hands were indeed busily engaged in tying his ankles. A wizened little face peeked up at him.

"Hello!" Angelo said merrily.

Mr. Morland screamed and fumbled at the door latch. "Stop the carriage right now! This moment!"

"Certainly, sir," Sir Belvedere's voice answered. "Your order is my command."

The carriage ground to a halt, and Mr. Morland finally got the door open and fell out onto the road. He pulled his still-speechless cousin with him, and the two of them ran as fast as they could into the darkness at the side of the road. Mr. Morland was forced to hop rather than strictly run, thanks to Angelo, but he was very fast nonetheless.

It was just as Louisa, Lady Lettice, and Sir Belvedere had planned.

Louisa laughed and laughed as she watched them fade away, the underbrush rustling until finally there was only silence. "Oh, I did enjoy that!" she said happily. "It was over much too quickly, though."

"Are you quite all right?" Lady Lettice asked. "We followed as quickly as we could, but we were not certain which direction you went in."

"I am perfectly well, even though that idiot tried to compromise me." Louisa put her head out to see Sir Belvedere sitting atop the box. "What happened to the coachman, Sir Belvedere?"

"Oh, we set him down about a mile past. He is sure to be at the village by now. He was so foxed I am sure he thought we were a hallucination. I am becoming an excellent driver, don't you think?"

"Superb," said Lady Lettice. "But if we sit about here all night, we shall miss the entire ball. I want to dance at least once."

"And so do I!" Louisa agreed heartily. She looked out the window as Sir Belvedere turned the carriage and set off toward the castle. "You do not think they will try to come back, do you?"

"Of course not. Didn't you see their expressions? They were frightened out of their wits. What little wits they possess, that is." Lady Lettice lifted up the little mirror at her belt and examined her coiffure. "I think, my dear Louisa, that we should resolidify before we reach the castle, if we want to dance without frightening all the guests."

"Forgive me, my lord, but I must speak with you," a footman said in a breathless voice, as if he had just run a great distance.

Phillip and Cassie were talking to Lady Royce, but their conversation ceased at this quiet interruption.

"Of course," said Phillip. "Is there some sort of trouble?"

"Trouble?" Cassie echoed. The only "trouble" she could think of was Mr. Bates. Could he have returned to ruin the ball?

"I think—I fear a lady may have been abducted," the footman gasped. "I saw her being carried away from the ball, down the drive. She dropped this before the man put her in a carriage, and they drove away." He held up a shepherd's crook, trimmed in now-bedraggled blue and yellow ribbons.

"That is my crook!" Cassie cried.

Phillip looked down at her, puzzled. "Your crook, my dear?"

"The one that went with my other costume. The costume I thought I saw someone wearing earlier." She turned to the footman. "Was the lady wearing a blue-and-yellow shepherdess gown?"

He shrugged helplessly. "I fear it was too dark to be sure, Miss Richards. She *was* wearing a light-colored bonnet."

"And the man with her?" Phillip asked.

"He was wearing a sort of hooded cloak, my lord. But I think there may have been two men there."

"*Two* men?" Cassie caught at Phillip's arm. "Mr. Bates and Mr. Morland, it has to be! They have come back."

"Why would you think that?" Phillip asked quietly. "Have you heard something from them?"

Cassie shook her head. "Not at all. But it sounds exactly like something they would do. Mr. Bates was not at all happy to be thwarted in the matter of my land. Oh, poor Louisa!"

"Louisa?" Aunt Chat said, coming up to their small group just in time to hear these last words. "Has something happened to Louisa?"

"I saw someone earlier, walking about dressed in my shepherdess costume," Cassie explained. "I am sure it was her. She left me this gown and took mine. Now Mr. Bates has snatched her, thinking it was me."

"How terrible!" Lady Royce said. "What if he does her harm?"

"Mother, Cassandra," said Phillip. "I do not wish to appear unconcerned about your friend, but how exactly can Mr. Bates hurt her? She is, er, no longer alive."

"I still do not like this," Cassie murmured.

"Let us go find them," said Phillip. "I'm not certain how long they have been gone, but they can't have gone far. I don't imagine Mr. Bates will care to keep traveling when he realizes his mistake! But I do not like the idea of Mr. Bates coming back to the castle to hurt you." His expression darkened. "I do not like it at all."

Cassie couldn't help a small shiver at the thought of being carried off by Mr. Bates. If Louisa had in fact taken her place, she owed her a great debt of gratitude. "Shall we go look for them, then?"

Phillip nodded. "Very well, but we will not go far. Mother, you and Lady Willowby stay here and make certain the ball goes on smoothly."

Lady Royce nodded. "What about your—important announcement?"

"We will make it when we return, with Louisa safely in tow."

So it was that Phillip, Cassie, and Antoinette set off down the drive, still clad in their costumes and armed only with torches and Antoinette's ankh-topped staff. But they did not have to go a great distance. A black, closed carriage, drawn by a coachman in clattering armor, turned in the gates just as they reached the end of the drive.

"Good eve to you!" Sir Belvedere cried, drawing up on the reins.

Louisa and Lady Lettice appeared at the window. "What are you all doing out here?" Lady Lettice said. "Is the ball over already?"

"Oh, it cannot be!" Louisa complained. "I have not had one dance yet."

"Are you all right, Louisa?" Cassie cried, running up to the carriage, her blue satin skirts held up above the gravel and dust. "Was it Mr. Bates who took you away?"

"Indeed it was," Louisa said. She opened the carriage door and stepped down onto the drive, shaking out her gown. "The cabbage-head. He tried to take some most indecent liberties." Then she laughed merrily. "Oh, but you should have seen his face when I revealed my identity! I do not think we will ever see him or his odious cousin again."

"Liberties?" Cassie said, dismayed. "Louisa! How terrible. I am so sorry."

Louisa gave her a puzzled look. "Why are *you* sorry, Cassie? You did not kidnap me."

"But I was the one he meant to take. If not for me, you would not have been put in such an unpleasant position."

Louisa shrugged. "What could he do to me? I am already dead! We were just happy there was something we could do for you, after all your kindness to us. Besides, it was vastly amusing."

Phillip stepped up to her and gave her a deep bow. "I can never thank you enough, my lady," he said softly, seriously. "I owe you a great debt of gratitude for saving the woman I love."

Louisa looked at him steadily. "I fear I always thought you were rather stuffy. Even as a child, you were so solitary, so intent on your purpose—like my husband. But now I know what a true and gallant heart you have. I am very sorry for all the silly tricks we have played on you over the years, like spilling your ink and disarranging your papers."

"And I, too, apologize, my lord," Sir Belvedere said, climbing down from the carriage box.

"*I* have nothing to apologize for," Lady Lettice said. "Do you, Angelo?"

"Not I!" Angelo's voice piped from the depths of the carriage.

"Then we should go back to the ball, before it is all over and done with," said Lady Lettice.

"I quite agree," answered Phillip. Then he put his arm around Cassie and smiled down at her. "We have a very important announcement to make."

Chapter Twenty-Five

Phillip stood in the center of a group of well-wishers, watching across the room as Cassie was enveloped and carried away by just another such group. Her cheeks were flushed and glowing from the excitement of the evening and the emotion of the announcement of their betrothal, and her eyes were shining like dark stars. She laughed at something Mr. Lewisham said to her, and the sweet sound seemed to hover over the chatter like a silvery cloud.

What a fortunate man he was, he thought, as all the crowd and noise seemed to fade away, leaving only her in his sight and senses. Only weeks before, he had been so solitary, concerned only with his work. Now a whole new life stretched out before him, beckoning him down a new road. A road of love and marriage, a place in a community, and, one day, a family. Children with Cassie's sparkling brown eyes and mischievous ways.

He was not certain he was exactly prepared for it, but he was looking forward to it. Very much.

"Congratulations, Lord Royce," someone beside

him said. "You are so fortunate to have gained the
hand of such a fine lady."

Peter looked over to see Sir Belvedere standing
there in his armor. "Thank you," he said. "She is
indeed a very fine lady."

"She rather reminds me of—of someone I knew
once, long ago," Sir Belvedere said.

They both watched for a moment as Cassie moved
through the crowd, with Antoinette on one side of
her and Lady Lettice on the other. Angelo trailed
behind them, holding a bowl of marzipan candies in
his hands and smiling down at them blissfully.

"I also wanted to thank you again for your actions
tonight," Phillip said. "You and Louisa and Lady
Lettice. It was very brave of you."

If Sir Belvedere had had the capability, Phillip was
certain he would have blushed. As it was, he shuffled
a bit in his armor, causing a great racket. " 'Twas
nothing at all, my lord. Why, what could such a
knave as Mr. Bates do to us!" He lowered his voice
and said confidentially, "We *are* already dead,
y'know."

"I know. That does not make it any less brave.
When Louisa allowed herself to be carried off in Cassandra's place, she saved her a great deal of fear and
pain. I will always be grateful for that."

"I know Louisa did not mind doing it at all. Truth
to tell, I think she found it rather exciting."

"I do wish you had let me know what was going
to happen. I could have assisted you."

Sir Belvedere shook his head. "We did not want
to trouble you, my lord. Especially on such an important night as this, with the announcement of your
betrothal."

"Nevertheless . . ." Phillip was interrupted when
his mother announced the last dance before supper,

the "Sir Roger de Coverley," which Phillip was meant to lead off with his new fiancée. Sir Belvedere melted into the crowd, and Phillip went to claim Cassie for the dance.

She took his hand, and let him lead her into their places in line, giving him the most brilliant smile Phillip had ever seen.

How Louisa had missed dancing! Her feet tingled with joy at moving through the familiar patterns again, and she hummed beneath her breath along with the tune. Oh, it *was* delightful! Truly the finest night she had known since the end of her mortal life.

Her partner, a rather portly Harlequin, twirled her about, and she skipped back to her place in line to await her next partner. When she spun around to meet him, she found herself holding hands with the Cavalier she had glimpsed earlier.

"William!" she whispered, stumbling a bit in her surprise. It had been almost one hundred and thirty years since she had seen her husband, but he had not changed a bit. "It *was* you I saw."

"Hello, Louisa," he answered in his deep, serious voice. Then he spun her back into her place in line and went on to the next lady.

Louisa's feet automatically carried her through the patterns of the dance, but she scarcely even glanced at her new partner. She twisted her neck about, trying to keep William in her sight, but he was always lost in the swirl of dancers.

Perhaps she had not really seen him. Perhaps she had only imagined seeing him again, after all this time.

But then she shook her head. That had not been imagination! She had truly seen William again, touched his hand. And it had been as jolting, as exalting, as it was at the ball where she had first met him.

The dance did not bring them together again. As soon as the music ended, she made her way through the tangle of people pairing off for supper. She searched every face carefully, and found three men costumed as Cavaliers, but none were William.

At last, she felt a soft, feather-light touch on her shoulder and looked up to see him there.

"William!" she cried. She went up on tiptoe to put her arms around his shoulders, burying her face in the familiar curve of his neck. His long hair tickled her cheek, as it always had when they kissed. "It is you. I knew it!"

"Yes," he said, his own arms coming about her waist, pulling her closer into him. "It is me."

"Where have you been all these years? Why did you move on and leave me here? Why did I have to stay so long?"

"So many questions," he said, his voice full of laughter. "You are still the same Louisa."

She pulled back to frown at him. "Do not make fun of me!"

He looked back at her steadily. "I would not do that."

"Would you not?"

"Of course not. We have been apart far too long for that. And as for your questions . . ." He looked about the still-crowded ballroom. "Come with me."

He drew her into the dim, deserted library and shut the door behind them. Louisa went and perched herself on the edge of Lord Royce's desk, and her husband came to stand beside her.

"We are all sent to Earth to learn something," he said. "It just took you a bit longer than some."

Louisa was puzzled. "What sort of lesson do we have to learn?"

"It is different for every person. But yours and mine were very similar."

"What was it?" As usual, William tried her quick-silver patience. But she was so very happy to see him again that it almost did not matter.

Rather than answer her question directly, William smiled and said, "We were in love when we married, were we not, Louisa?"

She thought back to those golden days of their courtship and wedding. "Oh, yes."

"Yet our downfall was that we were selfish people. We cared too much about ourselves and not enough about our marriage. After the king was restored to the throne, I should have come back to you. Instead, I stayed at Court, trying to gain favor. I left you alone here."

Well, not strictly alone, Louisa thought, tears prickling at her eyes. That had been the problem. The memory of those days still had the power to hurt her: the loneliness, the waiting. And the parties she had held here, trying to forget. "That was no excuse for my behavior."

"Perhaps not. But I am as much to blame for that as you were. Just as I was to blame for your death."

Louisa looked up at him, startled. "How so?"

He took her hand in his. "If I had been here, taking care of you as I should have, it would not have happened. We could have had children and a life together. That was the lesson I had to learn, and I learned it well when I heard that you had died. My lesson, and yours, was that only our love, our marriage, our time together, mattered. Not favor at Court, not wealth and land."

"But I always knew that!" Louisa cried, bewildered and touched, and very, very sad.

"No," William answered gently. "You knew that you were hurt, that I could not give you what you wanted. But you did not see that we as individuals were not so important—only the love we found was. And you realized that by helping Phillip and Cassandra to not make the same mistake."

Louisa thought back on so many things, on their own marriage, on the past few weeks with Phillip and Cassie. She had seen how very much they cared about each other and how they tried to deny that at first. Just as she had been denying her love for William ever since the night she drank too much brandy in her despair over him and went tumbling over the cliff.

And she now knew that what William said was the truth, and she had learned her lesson well. It had just taken her decades longer, that was all.

"You see now, do you not?" William whispered. "Cassandra is you, and Phillip is me. And you have helped them to have the chance that we never had, thanks to our own stubbornness."

"I see," Louisa said with a joyful smile. "I see perfectly." She turned her face up to his for a kiss she had been waiting one hundred and thirty years for.

When it was over, William looked at her solemnly and said, "Are you ready to go, then?"

"Oh, yes. I am ready."

Within seconds, the library was utterly deserted, as if no one had ever been there at all.

Except for two shadowy figures in the corner.

"Do you think she is gone forever?" Lady Lettice asked, staring at the spot on the desk where Louisa and William had just been. She would have thought she would be glad to see Louisa gone, to have the East Tower all to herself. But she found that she felt strangely bereft.

"Oh, I am sure she will come back to visit one day," Sir Belvedere said, reaching into his armor to produce a handkerchief, which he presented to her with a flourish. "She will not be able to resist giving us all the gossip from the other side."

"No doubt," Lady Lettice said. "And I am very happy she found her husband again. It is only . . ."

"Only what?"

"Well, I am not sure *I* will ever find my love again. Or if he was ever truly my love in the first place."

Sir Belvedere patted her hand. "You will. We just have to learn our lessons, as William said. And we are intelligent people. We can do that, I am sure."

Lady Lettice smiled at him. "I am sure we can."

"In the meantime, would you care for a card game in the East Tower, fair lady?"

"I would enjoy that. But first, I must snatch Angelo away from the refreshments."

"It was a lovely ball. The finest ever, I am sure," Cassie sighed, leaning on Phillip's arm as he led her up the staircase and down the corridor toward her chamber. She had imbibed just a tiny bit too much champagne at supper, and her heeled slippers wobbled.

The house was quiet now, with all the guests departed or tucked up in their chambers, and the first grayish light of dawn peeped in at the windows. But Cassie still felt like she could dance for hours more.

"It was a splendid ball," Phillip agreed. "Though I hope you will not want to go on having masked balls every year when we are married." He tugged again at the hem of his costume, as he had been doing all evening.

Cassie laughed. "If I do, you will not have to come as an ancient Greek again."

"Will I not?" he said hopefully.

"No. You could be an ancient Roman!"

"Such a great difference."

"Indeed there is." She stopped at the door to her room and leaned back against the sturdy wood, smiling up at him. "But I confess I rather like *this* costume."

"Then I will wear it again, though only for you."

"Hm, that sounds quite acceptable to me." She kissed his cheek. "Thank you for tonight. It was indeed splendid."

"A night worthy to tell our grandchildren about?"

"Undoubtedly."

"Yet also, I fear, a long one. You should be asleep. My mother and your aunt will want to get started with wedding plans later, I am sure."

"I am ready for anything! Even wedding plans." But then she broke into a large, uncontrollable yawn. "I *am* rather sleepy, though. Good night, Phillip dear."

"Good night, my love."

Cassie kissed him once more, then ducked into her chamber, closing the door softly behind her.

Only when she heard his footsteps fading down the corridor did she turn to face the room and see the note that lay on the floor, a white square against the dark blue rug. She knelt down to pick it up, her satin skirts puddling around her, and opened it right there.

She read the short message twice, a smile spreading across her lips. "Oh, Louisa," she whispered. "Good fortune to you, my friend. Good fortune."

Epilogue

Five Years Later

"Penelope! Where are you?" Lady Lettice called, picking her way over the pebbles of the beach to peek into the tunnel entrance. She heard a soft, childish giggle, but pretended to be completely befuddled. "Lady Penelope Leighton. You must come out right this moment, or I shall be forced to fetch your father."

Dark, glossy curls peeped out from behind an upturned, rotting fishing boat. Then the whole child popped up, brown eyes shining with excitement and dust smeared across her dainty pink dress.

"Here I am, Lady Lettice!" she sang. "I was hiding from you."

"Indeed you were. You are becoming far too adept at that." Lady Lettice moved cautiously into the tunnel and took little Penelope by the hand. She had not been in the tunnels since that day more than five years ago, when Antoinette had summoned her there. She was not at all certain that she wanted to be there now, but she had to keep a sharp eye on

Penelope. Cassandra and Phillip had entrusted her with their daughter's care this afternoon.

"I thought I told you to stay on the shore!" Lady Lettice said to the grinning child.

"Did you, indeed?" Penelope said ingenuously.

"You know that I did."

"Well, I thought this *was* part of the shore. Does it not have sand on the floor?" Penelope trailed one tiny slipper through the grit of the tunnel floor. "Just like the beach."

The child was too clever for her own good, Lady Lettice thought wryly. "How did you find this place?"

Penelope tugged away from her to peek into one of the old crates stacked along the walls. "The man told me."

"Man?" Lady Lettice said, puzzled. "Do you mean Angelo?"

Penelope giggled. "No! Angelo is *Angelo*. The man is just a man." She picked a stick up off the floor and used it to poke through the contents of the crate.

Lady Lettice looked warily over her shoulder to the dark depths of the tunnel. *A man.* Could it possibly be that Mr. Bates, who had disappeared from England so long ago, and, as they had heard later, disappeared from Jamaica as well, was here?

No, she reassured herself. Mr. Bates would not come back; there was nothing for him to gain. Cassie had long ago sold her land in Jamaica, and she was long married, with Penelope, Edward, and new baby Louisa.

But then—who was "the man"?

Lady Lettice did not see anyone, but she had a creeping feeling about the tunnels. She walked over to Penelope and pulled the child down from the crates.

"Come along, now," she said. "We ought to return to the castle."

Penelope's lower lip trembled. "I am not finished exploring yet!"

"It is almost time for tea. Do you not want some of Cook's special lemon cakes, which she has made just for you?" Lady Lettice knew the value of bribery when it came to the Leighton children.

Penelope eyed the crates, obviously measuring their charms against the lure of cakes. "May I come back later, Lady Lettice?"

"If your parents say you may," Lady Lettice relented. "Perhaps Sir Belvedere or your nursemaid will bring you."

Penelope smiled happily and slipped her hand back into Lady Lettice's. As they turned to leave, a man's deep voice stopped them.

"Lettice," it said. "*Ma belle chère* Lettice."

Lady Lettice turned around and felt her breath catch in her throat. She pulled Penelope close to her. "Jean-Pierre," she whispered.

"So you remember me?" he said, emerging fully from the shadows. After more than two hundred years, he was still handsome, as dark and dashing as a pirate. He grinned at her.

But Lady Lettice would not be lulled by a dashing smile and a French accent. Not again. "Of course I remember you," she snapped. "Unfortunately."

"That is the man I saw!" Penelope piped up, her voice muffled in the silk of Lady Lettice's gown.

Lady Lettice glared at Jean-Pierre. "So now you are using children in your schemes?" she said scathingly.

Jean-Pierre looked crestfallen. He held his elegant hands out to her beseechingly. "I would never have hurt her, *ma belle* Lettice. I merely wanted to bring you here, so I could talk to you."

Lady Lettice felt a tugging at her skirt and looked down to find Penelope watching her with melting dark eyes. "Please, Lady Lettice," she whispered. "He only wants to talk to you. And he is *so* handsome."

Lady Lettice's gaze snapped back to Jean-Pierre to see if he had heard that. He obviously had, as he was covering his laughter with his hand.

Lady Lettice frowned at him, and he instantly sobered. "What could we have to talk about?" she said. "I thought you said everything when you dashed off back to France."

"Please, Lettice," he said, taking a small step toward her. "All of that was not as it appeared. I have been waiting a very long time to explain to you. I may not have very long here. All I ask is that you listen to me, for half an hour, no longer. If you do not believe me, you need never see me again."

Lady Lettice could feel herself wavering, drawn in by the warm, musical cadence of his voice and by the lure of his words. It had been ever thus with him.

She glanced down at Penelope. "I cannot talk to you now," she said, keeping her tone stern and doubting. "I have to take Lady Penelope back to her parents."

"*Certainment*. But you will come back later?" he said hopefully.

"Perhaps." She turned around and walked with Penelope back to the entrance of the tunnel.

As she turned out into the bright sunshine, she heard him call, "Please come back, *ma couer*."

Lady Lettice smiled secretly. *My heart*.

"Are you finished packing yet, Cassie?" Antoinette asked, adding one last book to her own already full valise and snapping it shut.

Cassie knew she should be making the final decision on which gowns to take to Bath. They were
meant to leave tomorrow, so that Phillip could discuss his newest book with Aunt Chat's Philosophical
Society, and her trunk was not half-full. But she
could not resist leaving her task to bend over baby
Louisa's basket and tickle her soft little feet.

Louisa laughed and kicked out in infant joy.

"What a brilliant baby you are!" Cassie cooed. "So
tiny, but you are already laughing and smiling. You
know your mama, don't you? Yes, you do!"

Antoinette came over to peer into the basket, as
well, holding out her finger for Louisa to grasp. "She
knows her Aunt Antoinette, too! Though you know
that her nursemaid says it is only air bubbles that
make her laugh."

"That is not true! It is because she has such a
merry nature. Penelope is going to be a brilliant
scholar, like her father; Edward is going to be a great
horseman; and Louisa is going to be my sunshine."

There was a quick knock at the door, and Melinda
came in, holding a jewel case in her hand. Behind
her was little Edward, galloping on the stick horse
Sir Belvedere had made for him.

Edward was a handsome, sturdy little boy, and
very swift as he trotted about his mother's chamber.
Unlike his older sister, who had long been speaking
in full sentences by the time she was his age, he did
not have an extensive vocabulary. But he could say
"horsie," "saddle," "phaeton," and "Tattersall's"
beautifully, as well as doing a perfect imitation of a
horse's neighing.

He did this now as he galloped, reining in only to
give his mother and aunt kisses.

"Oh, my dears, I need your advice!" Melinda said.
"Which jewels should I take to Bath? I asked Eddy,

but the little darling is absolutely useless about fashion. He just wanted to put my emerald brooch on his horse's mane."

"Let us see," said Antoinette. She, Cassie, and Melinda sat down on Cassie's bed, and spread the baubles out over the counterpane.

They were debating the merits of amethysts and pearls when Penelope came dashing in, curls and ribbons flying wildly behind her. "Mama!" she cried. "Grandmama, Aunt Antoinette, you will never guess what I found on my walk!"

Edward galloped up to her. "Penny. Horsie."

"Yes, Eddy, your horse is beautiful," she said, pausing to pat her brother's horse on the head before she climbed up onto the bed beside her mother. "I saw a man in the tunnel."

"A man?" Startled, Cassie pulled Penelope into her arms, looking over her dark curls to where Lady Lettice hovered by the door. What sort of a man could her daughter possibly be seeing in the tunnel? "Who was it?"

"A Frenchman," said Penelope, obviously unconcerned. "He was dressed funny, in puffy pants and a short cloak. He wore an earring, like this one." She held up one of her grandmother's pearl drop earrings. "And he knew Lady Lettice. He called her *ma couer*. Mrs. King says that means 'heart,'" she said, quoting her new French teacher.

"Was it Jean-Pierre?" Antoinette asked Lady Lettice.

Lady Lettice gave her a sharp look. "Did you summon him, Antoinette?"

"Certainly not," Antoinette answered. "I have not summoned anyone since you and Angelo. I have been spending my time doing useful things, like studying herbs." And publishing a book of herbology, full of the healing properties of plants and recipes for making soaps and bath oils.

"Well, he is here anyway," said Lady Lettice.

"What does he want?" Melinda asked.

"I do not know. I did not stay to chat with him."

"He wants her to come back later," Penelope said helpfully. "He wants to explain everything to her. He said . . ."

"Yes, thank you, Penelope," Lady Lettice interrupted. "That is enough."

Penelope grinned.

"Will you talk to him?" Cassie asked Lady Lettice.

Lady Lettice shrugged carelessly, but she would not quite meet their eyes. "Perhaps. It would be—interesting to hear what he has to say."

"But even if you talk to him, you will not just—go, as Louisa did, will you?" Cassie asked. She rather liked having Lady Lettice's company. And the children adored her; they would howl with laughter whenever she did her walk-through-walls trick.

"Certainly not," Lady Lettice said. "Jean-Pierre and I are not like Louisa and her husband. William loved Louisa truly in the end. Jean-Pierre—well, I am not certain why he is here, but I do know that he does not love me."

With that, she turned and left the room, so agitated that she did not see Phillip standing there, and floated right over him.

Phillip studied the company gathered there and laughed. "Well! Is this a *soirée* and I am not invited?"

"Papa!" Penelope and Edward shouted. They both ran across the room and leapt on their father.

Phillip knelt down and kissed them both. "You two are behaving as if you have not seen me in a year, when it has only been since breakfast."

"It has been a very long time since breakfast, Papa," Penelope said.

"Indeed it has, my poppet." Holding a child under each arm, Phillip stood and faced the cluster of ladies.

"We were helping your mother decide which jewels to take to Bath," Cassie explained.

"And did you make a decision?" Phillip asked.

"Oh, yes!" Melinda said happily. "All of them. There is simply no predicting what sort of things we will be invited to in Bath. Now, I should go and be sure my maid has finished all my packing." She came and held out her hands for the children. "Why don't you come with your grandmama, Penny and Eddy, and help me."

When they were gone, Antoinette picked up baby Louisa's basket and carried it to the door. "I should finish my packing, as well. Louisa can advise me. One is never too young to learn about fashion," she said.

As soon as the door closed behind them, Phillip drew Cassie into his arms for a lingering kiss.

"Ah, alone at last," he murmured against her neck.

"Yes. I just love the subtle way Antoinette and your mother herded the children out the door." Cassie pulled him closer to her and leaned her head back with a blissful sigh as his teeth found her sensitive earlobe. "Not that I am not delighted, my dear, but why are you here? You usually work straight through to teatime."

He leaned away to gesture toward the papers he had dropped when the children came rushing at him. "I wanted to ask you your opinion on some of today's work. Or perhaps I should have asked Penelope. She can already name the entire pantheon of gods. But all of that can wait." He pulled her close again.

Cassie briefly debated whether she should tell him

about the return of Jean-Pierre, but then decided that that, too, could wait. She lost herself in his ardent kiss.

Children, work, Bath, ghosts—*all* that could wait. This time was just for them.

⓪ **SIGNET** (0451)

MARTHA KIRKLAND

Kirkland delivers "TOP NOTCH REGENCY ENTERTAINMENT." —*Romantic Times*

MISS WILSON'S REPUTATION   20587-1
A rakish lord conceals his true identity in hopes of getting a
lovely jewelry maker to look past his reputation—and see his
true heart...

MR. MONTGOMERY'S QUEST   20439-5
Charlotte Pelham knows that no one would hire a lady as a
walking tour guide. So she applies as one *Charles* Pelham—and is
eagerly accepted. Her journey promises to be an interesting one—
especially when a handsome stranger joins the group on a
mysterious quest of his own...

THE RAKE'S FIANCEE   20260-0
Fate casts a newly titled baron back into the life of the woman who
once rejected him. Does he truly desire revenge, or something
more passionate?

To order call: 1-800-788-6262

S628/Kirkland

Signet Regency Romances
from
DIANE FARR

FALLING FOR CHLOE
0-451-20004-7
Gil Gilliland is a friend—nothing more—to his
childhood chum, Chloe. But Gil's mother sees more to
their bond. And in a case of mother knows best, what
seems a tender trap may free two stubborn hearts.

ONCE UPON A CHRISTMAS
0-451-20162-0
After a tragic loss, Celia Delacourt accepts an
unexpected holiday invitation—which is, in fact, a
thinly veiled matchmaking attempt. For the lonely
Celia and a reluctant young man, it turns out to be a
Christmas they'd never forget...

"Ms. Farr beguiles us."—*Romantic Times*

To order call: 1-800-788-6262

Signet Regency Romances from

ELISABETH FAIRCHILD

"An outstanding talent."
—*Romantic Times*

CAPTAIN CUPID CALLS THE SHOTS
0-451-20198-1

Captain Alexander Shelbourne was known as Cupid to his friends for his uncanny marksmanship in battle. But upon meeting Miss Penny Foster, he soon knew how it felt to be struck by his namesake's arrow...

SUGARPLUM SURPRISES
0-451-20421-2

Lovely Jane Nichol—who spends her days disguised as a middle-aged seamstress—has crossed paths with a duke who shelters a secret as great as her own. But as Christmas approaches—and vicious rumors surface—they begin to wonder if they can have their cake and eat it, too...

To order call: 1-800-788-6262

PENGUIN PUTNAM INC.
Online

Your Internet gateway to a virtual environment with
hundreds of entertaining and enlightening books
from Penguin Putnam Inc.

*While you're there, get the latest buzz on
the best authors and books around—*

Tom Clancy, Patricia Cornwell, W.E.B. Griffin,
Nora Roberts, William Gibson, Robin Cook,
Brian Jacques, Catherine Coulter, Stephen King,
Ken Follett, Terry McMillan, and many more!

**Penguin Putnam Online is located at
http://www.penguinputnam.com**

PENGUIN PUTNAM NEWS

Every month you'll get an inside look at our upcom-
ing books and new features on our site. This is an
ongoing effort to provide you with the most
up-to-date information about
our books and authors.

**Subscribe to Penguin Putnam News at
http://www.penguinputnam.com/newsletters**